Journey to Mars: The Awakening

TIM CONLEY

Copyright © 2012 Tim Conley

All rights reserved.

ISBN:1-4791-0668-2
ISBN-13: 978-1-4791-0668-4

DEDICATION

This book is dedicated to my son, James David (JD) who provided the spark for the creation of the Journey to Mars series as we spoke over a McDonald's Happy Meal one summer day way back in 2003. JD's keen mind had figured out that we already have the technology to get us to Mars. He just wondered when we were going to get there. Thanks, Son!

CONTENTS

	Acknowledgments	i
1	Chapter 1	1-6
2	Chapter 2	Pg #7-13
3	Chapter 3	Pg #14-17
4	Chapter 4	Pg #18-23
5	Chapter 5	Pg #24-28
6	Chapter 6	Pg #29-35
7	Chapter 7	Pg #36-39
8	Chapter 8	Pg #40-43
9	Chapter 9	Pg #44-46
10	Chapter 10	Pg #47-49
11	Chapter 11	Pg #50-55
12	Chapter 12	Pg #56-61
13	Chapter 13	Pg #62-66
14	Chapter 14	Pg #67-71
15	Chapter 15	Pg #72-76
16	Chapter 16	Pg #77-85
17	Chapter 17	Pg #86-92
18	Chapter 18	Pg #93-98
19	Chapter 19	Pg #99-103
20	Chapter 20	Pg #104-107

JOURNEY TO MARS: THE AWAKENING

21	Chapter 21	Pg #108-113
22	Chapter 22	Pg #114-118
23	Chapter 23	Pg #119-123
24	Chapter 24	Pg #124-129
25	Chapter 25	Pg #130-133
26	Chapter 26	Pg #134-137
27	Chapter 27	Pg #138-141
28	Chapter 28	Pg #142-147
29	Chapter 29	Pg #148-151
30	Chapter 30	Pg #1152-157
31	Chapter 31	Pg #158-165
32	Chapter 32	Pg #166-171
33	Chapter 33	Pg #172-177
34	Chapter 34	Pg #178-179

ACKNOWLEDGMENTS

Thank you to my wife, Carmela and my son, JD for sticking by my writing for all these years..

1 ARTIFICIAL DOCTOR IN A BOX

Instrument panels blurred as Jason tried once more to focus. The pain behind his eyes still caused him to squint. 'I can't hit that damned docbot for anything else.' he murmured to himself as he looked across the mission cockpit to where the rest of his crew lay in stasis, some of them permanently.

Jason rubbed his eyes again and returned his gaze to the panels. His mind also jerked back to the reason he was here. Here being about half way between Mars and Earth, on the return leg of a four-month journey that wasn't going to end too soon. He caught part of his expression in the Plexiglas cover on the bio status panel. Even with the distortion, he could still see the haggard look, which had become his face. Several days of stubble dotted his once rugged features. Hollowness around his eyes reminded him of how weary he actually felt. 'Bone-assed tired was the phrase she used.' At the moment he couldn't even remember who the she was.

He looked at the survival pods again and wondered why NASA couldn't get the mix right. Even after seventy-five years of trying they were still woefully lacking in putting together viable crews for long-range missions. But six occupied stasis chambers were clear testimony to the root of their troubles.

Boredom. Sheer backbreaking, mind-numbing boredom. That was Jason's take on the entire issue. He remembered Tom Broderick, from the first Mars mission. Tom had required extensive hospitalization following his return to Earth. His emaciated body was one thing but Tom had once had one of the best minds in NASA.

When Jason had visited him there was no one home. It was almost as if someone had lobotomized his friend. Tom had barely held his crew together long enough to get them through a very complex approach to the Space Complex Moon facility. As it was rescue crews had taken two full days to reach the crew. Tom and Spence Richards were the only ones still alive out of a crew of seven. And NASA called the mission a success.

The second mission had gone slightly better. Perhaps they had assembled the right mixture of crewmembers. They had missed their return window by five weeks because of a meteor storm that had pounded the surface of Mars and there were those who said the challenges of salvaging the mission had worked to heighten their sense of mission importance. Each member was closely monitored for months before NASA officials finally gave the thumbs up for Mission III.

Jason now wished they hadn't. He earnestly wished he hadn't been so gung-ho when they told him he had been selected as the mission commander. He desperately wanted to forget that he had handpicked his crew. Of the seventeen candidates he had personally narrowed the field down to eight.

Four men and four women, two of them from Canada, a Russian from the Ukraine, an Australian, and four from the good old US of A. Their credentials had been impeccable, their service records spotless and Jason had served with each of them during the buildup of the various parts of the Moon Base.

Now seven of them occupied heated, insulated beds encased in that special plastic the defense industry had developed to ward off radiation. Two of the cases were doing their thing at the deep freeze level. Tony Benedict had been killed on Mars and Marsella Reid by something they hadn't been able to diagnose.

One morning after take-off she had started to bleed profusely from her mouth. The ship's medical personnel, Amanda Blake and Harvey Keith could do nothing. A brief autopsy revealed she had picked up a fungus on the surface that had consumed her lung tissue. Jason knew they had to take her back for the doctors to study. They had to know what they were dealing with.

The other crewmembers had become lethargic following her death. It seemed the Commander had been the soul of the crew. She had managed to pull them together during the training phase of the mission. Marsella had delivered the eulogy for Tony after they recovered his body from the rockslide. No one said anything about it but Jason knew they were thinking he had lost his command during that incident.

'You're not thinking coherently, buddy.' He was aware that he had begun to talk to himself instead of aloud. The entire crew had discovered that their SCAT (Space flight Cognitive Assessment Tool) was very sensitive to vocal utterances. Jason knew he had begun sub-vocalizing during the leg out from Earth. He hadn't wanted to go through the series of useless puzzles and tests that SCAT used to diagnose how he felt. "I knew how I felt!" he shouted. He saw SCAT's panel light up. "I don't need your meddling into my brain to know what is wrong!"

SCAT started to ask him how he felt, but Jason turned off the audio. He didn't need to listen to canned drivel to know he wasn't feeling up to par. His body felt so heavy and he didn't want to move. Depression. Extreme depression was his diagnosis. It was also the same thing Major Keith had said just before he passed out. Jason had to struggle to get him into his couch. It felt as if he didn't have the energy to get back off the command chair to check on the crew's state.

Jason looked at SCAT again. The crystal led was flashing an urgent message. It would continue until Jason turned on the audio and answered the questions or until they hit the Earth's atmosphere. No matter how sophisticated they made a computer, it was still just a computer, without a soul. Without true understanding.

That was where NASA had truly screwed up Mission III. They had again thought too highly of their newfound technology. "Fuck technology!" Jason screamed and pounded his fists against the command console. Technology was not going to get any of them home in time to make this mission successful. It was not going to answer those questions NASA really wanted answered. Beyond a fungus that ate lung tissue they had found nothing. And it could have been something dormant carried with them from Earth.

Nothing but questions. Brain numbing questions and few answers, if any. Jason felt too tired to make it his survival couch. He didn't think he could get his brain to function enough to get him halfway through the process that might save his life. He tried to get up but his body wouldn't cooperate. Besides, a thought occurred to him. At least one of them had to be awake to bring them into the Moon's orbit. Someone had to put the brakes on. The crew had somehow voted that he would be the one.

2 ROMANTIC INTERLUDE

Jason stepped out of his sports car and glanced up at the Moon. It was full. Halloween was less than a week away and Molly already had the kids geared up to enjoy all the festivities. She always paid close attention to what they would wear, where they would go and how much candy they would be allowed to eat following their rampage through the neighborhood. She even knew which houses the kids could and couldn't visit.

Their house was lit up with candles in the windows already. Two huge, carved pumpkins were sitting on the porch watching his approach. Missy and Alex heard his tread on the boards leading up to the door of the old house Molly was spending most of her time remodeling. The door popped open and they squealed and shouted for him to pick them up.

Why Molly had insisted on having them so close together still amazed him. Missy was barely a year old when Alex was born. She was now six and kept her mother running. Of course, Alex had to do everything, or at least try to do everything his sister was doing. So now he was jumping up and down wanting daddy's attention.

Jason hauled both of them into the house with him and kissed Molly as she came to meet him. Even after two kids and a huge remodeling project she still looked good. Her firm body pressed against him as the kids transferred their affection for a brief moment from dad to mom.

He felt interested in spite of the fact they had decided not to have another child until after the mission was completed. Molly saw the look pass through his eyes and held up a finger. "Jason Martin, that was in no way an encouragement for your wanton lusts." She smiled and walked back into the kitchen, looking back over her shoulder as she went. The sway in her hips said she was glad he was home.

Jason sat the kids down in his easy recliner and looked toward the kitchen. He really wanted to go in there and slide up behind her. She sometimes liked to 'do the dirty' while she washed dishes, but the kids had to be in bed for that to happen. Jason sighed and concentrated on listening to the two rascals lodged deep into his chair. "Daddy, you gotta see me in my ninja. Momma put up my sword until Holloweeny"

"Well she should have, Champ. And who told you to call it that?" Jason raised his eyebrows at his daughter. Everything Alex did always started with her. She blushed and shrugged her small shoulders. "Penny down the street said that is what it is." was her defense. Jason was about ready to let her know it was rude but was interrupted by Molly from the kitchen.

"You kids need to wash those hands. Supper is ready." Jason realized how famished he was as the kids rushed toward the bathroom. The smells coming from the kitchen really got his juices flowing. He waited on the kids and entered the dining room with them.

Molly had been doing some more paintwork in one corner of the dining room so the table was pushed over away from the walls. Jason detected the turpentine smell but it was driven out his nostrils as Molly opened the serving dish and let out the aroma of oven-fried game hens.

Supper passed very pleasantly. Jason reveled in the conversation. Molly liked to keep him up on the children's progress. She was convinced they were old enough for pre-school, but their birthdays being in December meant that Missy was going to have to wait another year. Of course, Alex was going to try whatever his sister did so Molly had to develop a program for both of them. "They're going to make you proud," she was saying.

Jason jerked awake and looked sheepishly across the table. Molly was trying to cover the fact that she had caught him drifting in and out of the conversation. "I can show you their curriculum later, or not." she left things hanging.

Flushed red by now, Jason excused himself. "Training has my mind going in twenty different directions," he stammered, but she didn't need him to tell her that. After eight years of marriage she was aware of when he began to lose his attention span. Some nights he barely made it past the main course before his mind was on something else, usually work related.

Molly sighed and bent over to hug his neck as she cleared dishes from the table. Jason patted her arm and looked up into the clearest eyes he had ever seen. Her eyes had completely captivated him as they were dating. He had felt at times like he could fall in and completely lose himself. That feeling came back full force and the words of a song suddenly jumped into his head 'need a heart with four-wheel drive…' as he looked up at her. "Honey, I love you very much," he whispered as she held him.

She smiled and kissed him gently on the lips. "There's more of that once the dishes are finished," she promised. "Can I get you to get the kids ready for bed?" He nodded and watched her carry dishes into the kitchen. 'How did I ever get so lucky?' he asked himself.

Alex already was running for the bathroom as Jason rose from his chair. He knew that getting ready for bed meant taking a bath. Bath was spelled with capital letters where his little brain was concerned. Molly often remarked that he would look like a prune if she didn't monitor him.

Jason followed him into the bathroom and grabbed his Discover magazine on the way. Maybe he could get some reading in while the kids splashed and squealed. He started their bath and then lost himself in several articles as they played. It might have gone on forever except for Molly's insistence that they had been in the tub long enough. Jason got them dressed for bed and was finishing Thomas the Tank Engine when Molly leaned on the door.

"They're already asleep?" she sounded a little disappointed but it swiftly passed. She got very little time to spend with her husband and she wanted to maximize every moment. She put her arms around his neck as he turned off the overhead light and softly pulled the door almost shut, leaving just a crack. Both kids wanted the hall light left on.

Jason looked intensely into her face that was raised so close to his. "I still haven't figured out why you chose me out of all those eligible studs on campus, Mrs. Martin. Can you enlighten me?"

Molly shook her head probably for the hundredth time. Her motivation to love Jason Martin had occurred on so many different levels that she didn't understand it herself. How was she to tell the man she loved just one thing when she knew it was so much more? She smiled and raised her lips to his. Moments passed as they explored the sensuality level. Both knew it was going to become intense.

"I'm going to take you right here. Against the door!" he stated as he felt the heat rise in an area south of his belt. She laughed and backed away from him. "And let your children know what it is you do with their mother?" her tone was mocking as she ducked under his Frankenstein's monster arms. He changed suddenly into Dracula and lunged for her but she slipped out of his grasp and ran frightened toward their bedroom.

He blocked the door as she tried to slam it closed and grabbed her around the waist. "I will rip all your clothes from your worthless body before I drink you blood," he stated as she appeared to faint and slump onto the bed.

Jason looked down at his wife and knew what she wanted to happen next. She liked being taken as she lay there helpless. She would awaken slowly during the process and her fist beat upon Jason's chest as she tried to get him to stop, but it was too late for stopping anything. He was already deep within her and her body was already responding as it always did with a rising passion that seared his soul to its core.

To him, Molly's passion was lifted from the deepest pools. She made him feel completely like a man. No, she made him feel more than that. She touched his soul every time they made love and this time was no exception.

More than an hour passed as they explored each other sexually. Jason was dripping with sweat as he lay on the bottom and watched her ride his still hard penis. Her wedding ring dug into his fingers as she tightly grasped his hands. The thrust from her pelvis was coming faster and faster. Jason watched closely as the skin around her neck and face began to mottle and change color. She was beginning to orgasm and Jason let her know he approved. "Let it come, baby!"

Molly's head snapped back and she moaned and softly screamed. Moments passed and Jason joined her with his own ejaculation. She finally leaned forward and tried to rest against his body but his continued thrusting upwards sent thrills through her. "Jason, let me rest." she moaned, then joined him in meeting his thrusts. Her head seemed to explode as another orgasm rushed over her. Her lips found his again and she kissed him as if it might be the final time.

Later she placed her head on his chest and drifted off the sleep in the only position she truly liked. His arms were around her as he felt himself drifting along on the cloud that preceded deep sleep.

His body and soul were extremely satisfied. His mind was released by the passion. He floated above the bed and looked down on sheets and bedclothes that were rumpled, at bodies that couldn't get much closer together and watched as his dear wife slept peacefully.

Morning sun slipping through the cracked window his wife had opened after she arose to check on the kids. Years of marriage had taught her that he liked fresh air first thing in the morning. She had even planted her herb garden outside their bedroom window so hints of rosemary could come through with the sunshine.

Jason awoke slowly and breathed deeply. Molly's scent was still warm on the bedclothes. He settled back into the bed and listened to her singing in the kitchen. She had the TV tuned to TNN.

'I guess it's true.' he thought, 'you can't take the country out of the girl.' Jason smiled and drifted back asleep for a moment. But Molly wasn't going to let him sleep in. She was at the door asking him something…

She was saying. She was saying…no, it wasn't quite right. She wasn't saying. Jason's head jerked up and he wiped his mouth with the back of his hand. His eyes still burned but they would focus. He reached over to the comms panel and turned up the volume.

"This is Moon Base Control. Come in Mars Explorer III. This is Moon Base Control. Come in Mars Explorer III. This is…" Jason switched it off. He could tell from the inflection that it was a recorded piece designed to get the crew's attention. The only problem being that he no longer had a crew. His comm officer was in the deep freeze and the only one left was him. He didn't want to talk with Moon Base Control yet.

'There's not enough to tell them.' he lied to himself. Actually there was plenty to tell them, he just didn't want to have to explain himself. He rubbed the stubble on his face again and shook his head. He looked across the cabin and could almost see the table set by Molly.

He withered inside and wanted to cry that it wasn't fair. How could she be so real? She had really been haunting his dreams since lift-off. His fists balled up and he slammed them into the console. Unfortunately the impact jarred the medical-examiner.in-a-box.

"Commander, please answer the following questions to the best of your ability…"

Jason stabbed at the button. The cabin rang with the departing decibels and suddenly the thought of having no one to carry on a real conversation with was more than he could bear. He opened the relay and heard the acknowledgement message pass back to Moon Base Control. Minutes passed as the message made its way across the distance. He jumped as Colonel O'Keefe voice came out of the speakers.

"Commander Martin, this is Moon Base Control. Colonel O'Keefe speaking. Is your crew ready for their debrief?"

3 29 MINUTES VS. 32

SCAT's alarm panel was lit up. Alarm bells should have chimed throughout the cabin. Jason was tempted to reach under the panel and disable SCAT's logic. But he didn't. Colonel O'Keefe had ordered him to take the full battery of tests. 'They don't know how bone weary I am.' he grouched.

Jason had just spent two hours of delayed conversations with O'Keefe and the medical staff boys, detailing what he could remember from the mission. "You've left some very big holes there," said the Colonel. "We want you to go back and take it from the top. Can you do that?"

"I'll try."

"First thing we need you to do is run through SCAT's test bank. I don't mind telling you Commander. We are pretty concerned with your mental state. Tell me again about the lift-off from Mars surface. Was there a reason you did it on your own? How many of your crew were functional at that time?"

Jason placed his head in his hands and tried to think. Why couldn't he accurately remember all the facts? They were facts, weren't they? His mind seemed so jumbled. One day seemed to have run into another.

"How many days ago was that?" he asked. Minutes passed as he waited for them to inform him of the event horizon. He tried to count back, and then remembered that the computer would have all the data he needed. His mind was starting to work again. He shoved his seat forward and reached across to the main computer board. He felt his adrenal glands kick in. Fingers that had been lethargic just a couple hours earlier started flying across the keypad.

"26 days, 11 hours and 29 minutes from liftoff." was the readout above the computer's data entry keypad. 'Why didn't I look at that before?' he wondered. Jason suspected the answer as soon as his brain presented the question. His cognitive functions had shut down. Extreme boredom had worked its way very firmly into his system.

"Commander, this is Kim Wang." a female voice sounded load and clear from the speaker. "We have liftoff at 26 days, 11 hours and 32 minutes elapsed time. Do you concur?"

"Negative, Control. Liftoff occurred at 29 minutes, not 32. Again, liftoff occurred at 29 minutes versus 32." Jason scratched his head. 'Why the difference?' He knew all about the imaging devices that had been trained on their habitat. He had helped set that up. There was no way that Earth should have the event horizon off by 3 minutes.

O'Keefe came back on the line. "Commander Martin, can you account for those three minutes? Did you have a power flux or anything anomalous during takeoff that might account for it?"

Jason tried to think, then turned his attention to the computer's audit trail. Entering the date information he retrieved and keyed information to Moon Base Control. They were seeing the same data that he was looking at. He looked through time hack after time hack. All systems were dumping data into the trail. 'There is no anomaly.'

Finally he pushed his seat back and stood up. Coldness had settled into the pit of his stomach that he couldn't dismiss. 'It is possible that someone or something has manipulated that data.' was his conclusion. 'But that means there's something going on here that I wasn't supposed to think about.'

Jason looked around the cabin again. Nothing looked out of the ordinary, but he wasn't sure what it was he was looking for. Whatever it turned out to be would appear normal. He was beginning to feel paranoid.

Jason reached over and flipped on SCAT's controls again. Right now he wanted answers. Answers to basic questions about how he felt, how far off his reactive times were; a whole host of things that would give him a benchmark.

Several hours passed before Moon Base Control interrupted his train of thought. "Mars Mission III, this is Moon Base Control. Commander, this is Howard Bernstein. How are you holding up?"

Jason looked sharply at the comm panel, and then relaxed. He had at least four minutes before they would want an answer. He still didn't know how he was feeling. SCAT had been processing his data for about fifteen minutes. It usually didn't take that long but it was probably trying to correlate today's answers with the last time he had taken the battery of tests. He was prepared to wait a while.

"Moon Base Control, this is Mars Mission III, I'm still waiting for SCAT's analysis. Is the Colonel still there?"

"Negative. He turned in a couple hours ago. Do I need to wake him?"

Jason thought about it for several minutes. "No. This is something that can wait. Listen, Howard. Do you have the tapes of the debrief from Mission II? Can you get your hands on them?"

"Sure. What in particular are you looking for on them? Maybe we can narrow the field for you if you can tell us what you're looking for."

"That's just it. I have no idea what it is. I just remember Commander Wilson talking about feeling bad all the way back. Can we start with that?"

"Roger, I'll download that for you as soon as we can. Is there anything else?"

"No, I guess not. I'm just curious about any correlations between their mission and this one."

The comm panel stayed silent, then Jason noticed a data transmission had started. It would probably take a couple hours to finish. Jason decided to get something to eat in the meantime. He had started to get up when SCAT finally finished his analysis.

"Commander Martin." the tinny voice grated on Jason's nerves. "Please acknowledge my greeting."

"You are acknowledged. SCAT. What are the results? Am I sane?"

"Commander. Analysis of your data indicates possible serious mental aberrations have occurred since the last time data was collected. Severe depression, anxiety, and psychomotor retardation are the most alarming. I'd like to monitor your mood and cognition for the next 24 hours.

4 CONTACT

Sand settled back into the ravine as the Mars Mission III personnel Lander powered down and rested on the quadrapod legs that supported its weight. Commander Jason Martin led his crew through the shut down process.

Meanwhile, something stirred within the sandy soil surrounding the Lander. Conscious stirrings that hadn't known anything for millennia upon endless millennia tensed as rare moisture started to coagulate and mix with red sand. Enzyme contacted enzymes long exposed to the elements. Like a virus long dormant it took many ticks of man's time for the being to even approach the point of active consideration of its situation.

Consider it did. Several hundreds of man's years had passed since even a small portion of the being's essence had escaped the red planet. Much preparation had gone into the cycle that sent spores to Earth with the last meteor bombardment. The being could now feel emanations coming from the third planet.

At least a portion of his essence had survived entry into the atmosphere. What form it had taken was beyond the being's ability to comprehend. That it probably resembled the life forms in the mechanical contraption resting on his planet was logical.

He suddenly felt bloodlust course through the body that was

forming within his sandy incubator. The beings needed to hurry up and disembark. He needed the heat of blood. Dirt began to crumble and settle around his succubus form. He could actually feel the wind of Mars begin to flake silica from his body.

Coldness alone existed on this cursed planet. Light from a distant sun gave no heat at all. Impatience grew as the being waited for the hatch to open. His period of dormancy had been so long, too long.

The being scanned the surface of his planet as he waited for the humans. None of the splendid edifices of his civilization remained. Sand and rock remained. His gaze traveled the length and breadth of Mars searching for anything that remained of his world. It was as the elders had predicted. Any water that remained on the planet was buried deep. Where shallow oceans had once been red sand now washed across barren landscape. No delicate spires rose above furled sails rocking to the delicate motions of calm seas. Brightly colored pennants no longer stirred with the gentle breeze blowing off Escarpment Heights.

A deep sadness depressed the being's new-formed body back into the sand. Impatience mounted as bloodlust became stronger.

It wouldn't be long and the bloodlust would be the only thing he would think about. Could think about. His body needed new blood to flow through his veins. He needed rich nourishment to flesh out his body. Tissue must be reformed. He was still weak, too weak to do what must be done. He realized patience, true patience, was necessary. That and stealth. He knew that now.

The hatch had opened. The beings coming through it didn't resemble anything he had ever seen. A hard carapace surrounded each of them. It wasn't at all like the soft-celled beings reported by those already upon the third planet.

The being reconsidered. How to attach itself to one of those hard shells became paramount in his thought patterns. He had to find a way, and soon. Bloodlust consumed him as he watched five of them walk past his resting place.

He turned his attention to their craft. The outer hatch had already closed. Two beings remained on board. They were also enclosed in their hard shells. He was too weak to reach their minds with his. He couldn't feel their thoughts. No use there. Bending their minds to his would take time. Time he didn't have.

He considered. There had to be some sort of communications between those on the surface and the ones still in the craft. He began to scan the electromagnetics and was satisfied by radio wave fluctuations. The strength of them nearly exploded inside his head before he filtered out most of their strength.

"Roger, there is nothing but sand out here. I'm going to collect a bit and then return to the Lander."

"Acknowledged. Mars Lander standing by. You have twelve minutes remaining on this walk cycle. UV radiation is off the scale, Commander. We don't want anyone out there for any longer than is necessary."

"Roger. We copy." Commander Martin looked around him. His crew was fanning out to cover as much territory in the small amount of time they had allotted for this first mission walk. He held the quadracam that recorded their every movement. 'This sure is a desolate place,' he thought.

"It is now," Bartam finished the thought. "You should have seen it during my day. This place was hopping." Bartam shut up as Commander Martin swiveled his head about. 'He heard me,' gasped Bartam. He waved his hand in a dismissive manner and the commander resumed his close attention of his crew, but there was something disturbing shaking the back of his mind.

Bartam melted back into the background and watched as the

crew continued their exploration of his home. They fanned out, each taking in a quadrant surrounding the landing site. None of them were ever out of sight of the others and their commander had them on film the entire cycle. Nothing within eyesight would be missed.

The crew approached the Lander. "Commander, this place gives me the creeps," Tony remarked as he placed his right boot on the bottom magnet strip of the ladder leading into the Lander. "I don't know about the others, but I feel like something is watching me."

He patted the firearm he wore at his side. "Something bugs me, like when you're getting ready for a fire fight in the jungle. Can't see anything, but you still know it's there."

"Noted, soldier," Commander Martin placed his hand on Tony's back, half in support as Tony climbed back toward the hatch. He looked around himself and didn't see anything. He also had that feeling Tony described. "What do you make of it?" he asked Angela as she approached.

"It's probably just nerves, Commander. I suggest he takes first turn with SCAT as soon as he decontaminates. We have a long time down here, so we need to watch what pushes our buttons," she concluded as she climbed. *'I'm not sure they should have sent a GI Joe with us,'* she thought silently.

Commander Martin continued his sharp-eyed observations as the entire crew climbed back on board. His feeling of dissatisfaction was still strong as he went into the UV chamber and locked the outer airlock. Green light washed over his suit and the suit sparkled briefly as ultraviolet did its job. His suit tingled as sound waves combined with the UV in ensuring nothing foreign was going to enter the crew's quarters. Jason finally hung up his suit and joined the crew.

"Two minutes to debrief," he drawled. Angela's head snapped up. "Commander, I've been with you for almost ten years and you don't drop back into your Texan accent unless you're disturbed by something. What gives?"

He shrugged and sat in the Command Chair. He glanced out the portal at the now distant Mars landscape before he answered. "I think Tony might have been right," was all he said. She allowed him to be alone with his thoughts. He finally snapped out of them as the others took their briefing places.

"Ok, we made it through the first walk cycle. Tony, your hackles were up out there. Did SCAT support your heightened awareness?"

Tony nodded enthusiastically. "Sure did. The profile matched those stored. Something tripped my trigger. The only time I've felt just like that was right before a fire fight." He stretched his arms over his head and looked very frustrated. Angela watched him closely.

The Commander was looking at her.

"Any ideas?" he asked. She shook her head for a moment. "We saw nothing out there, but I'm interested in why you are putting so much emphasis on how Tony felt out there. Did something trip your trigger too?"

A flutter of laughter went around the room, but stopped as everyone noted his reaction.

"Yes, Angela. Something did. I can't place my finger on it and that bothers me even more. Let's continue with the debrief and I'll consult SCAT as soon as we finish."

Outside, the object of their observations lay back down in its grave and waited. Bartam had observed a lot during the crews first time out on the planet. His observations included the ultraviolet bath the crew took on going back inside.

'That is going to be troublesome. I'm going to have to find a way of getting in there.' He lay back on the cold sand and contemplated as he rested.

5 OVERHEAD SHOTS

"Commander, this is Natasha," the link with the Mars Orbiter caught Jason's attention. He slid fully into his command chair and returned her greeting. That she hadn't used voice comms told him she wanted his attention alone. Her Russian upbringing and training almost required she follow a strict chain of command.

"What do you have?" flashed on her screen.

"Commander, put your headphones on so we can talk privately. This is going to take some explaining."

Jason frowned as he put on his headset. His crew would hear his half of the conversation but he didn't think any of them were paying attention. Astrid, Amanda and Tony were already asleep. Buzz was busy with an onboard experiment, getting ready to take the first part of their habitat outside. Harvey and Marsella were involved in a chess match that they had been playing since they left Moon orbit. Jason spoke softly into the mike, "What do you have, Nat?"

"Commander, there's no easy way to say this. You're setting directly on top of an anomaly in Mar's surface. One that wasn't there before you landed," she allowed a pause between her utterances.

"What kind of anomaly are we talking about?" he inquired, craning his neck to gaze out the window again. Something was niggling at the back of his mind again. "Can you pinpoint the location?"

"Yes, you are sitting right on top of it. Or rather, them. There are now two areas of atomization fluctuation outside the Lander."

"Distance from the Lander?"

"Roughly forty yards. Both appear to be about sixty-eight inches long by twenty-four inches wide. Commander, I'd describe them as bodies. I know that is absurd, but there appears to be a head, torso and legs in the outline. I'm sending you some overhead shots to your console now."

"Roger, I'm getting it now," Jason answered as he gazed at the overhead shots she was sending to him. A cold sensation settled into the pit of his stomach as the resolution became crisp. "There is definitely something there," he admitted. A something about the size of a man. "But how can that be? We were just out there and didn't see anything!"

"All I know, Commander, is what I saw this morning before you landed. Those scans are coming to you now. I've passed directly over you twice now since touchdown and both times there was something in the sand. This time it is very distinct."

Jason allowed the scans to download completely. No need to zoom in on the Lander's location. He could see the difference. One lump had appeared right outside the airlock and the other was directly behind the Lander.

"Nat, do you see any other lumps anywhere around us?"

"Negative, Commander. Only those two at the moment. I've been scanning out to a distance of ten miles, narrowing the scan at half-mile intervals. Nothing yet."

"Keep scanning," Jason hesitated for a few moments, looking closely at the lumps outside. He then twisted around and powered up the outside cameras. As their resolution settled he muttered to himself.

"What did you say, Commander?" came through his headset.

"Oh, I was just cursing myself for not having the cameras on already. They were the next set of instructions after our briefing. Should have moved them ahead in the priority list. Nat, let me know if anything else occurs with the 'lumps'. I'm going to try to focus on the one directly in front of us."

Jason called Buzz over and pointed at his screen. Buzz's eyebrows jerked upwards. "Holy shit! Tony had reason to be riled up, huh?"

Marsella had followed Buzz to the Command Console. "That looks human."

Jason looked at the expression on her face for a moment. "We better go to DefCon3," he stated bluntly. "Wake our sleepers and get everyone into their suits." He switched on his mike. "Natasha, monitor the lumps closely. Let me know if there is anyone movement or variation in either of them."

"Roger, Commander."

Buzz was now gazing sharply through the forward cameras. "I don't see a thing. Even infrared is blank."

"Take camera 3 through its entire spectrum," Jason instructed as he began struggling into his space suit. He looked at Amanda as she emerged from the sleep chambers. "Sorry to get you up, Number 2, but we have something for you to analyze."

"Roger, Commander." Amanda put the analysis off until she was dressed. The only thing she would need to do was snap the faceplate down. "Are these all the photos?" she inquired. She then fell silent. Except for the movement of fellow crewmembers the cabin was silent. When she looked up Amanda realized they were all waiting on her.

"This looks like a body of some sort," she stated flatly. "But we saw nothing out there. Was it there?"

Jason nodded. "It was there right after the Lander touched down. Natasha went overhead twenty-three minutes after we landed. That second set of photos come from that time frame. We've got to assume something is waiting out there for us."

"But why didn't it jump up while we were out there?" someone asked.

"I think it might have tried," Tony said matter of factly. "I told you I felt something."

Buzz interjected with a thought that was on everyone's mind. "What's it made of? I haven't seen anything you could make a body of."

"Sand." They all looked at the comms console. Natasha repeated herself as the orbiter reached the edge of terminus and passed out of range. "S-a-a-n-n-d-d." reverberated from the speaker.

Jason couldn't help the eerie feeling that vibrated up his spine. No one spoke until he reached over and turned down the gain on the speaker. The hiss and pops and cracks of deep space seemed to stay behind like an echo.

"Did she say sand?" Buzz asked. "I've never heard of anything being formed out of sand except for kids' castles."

Jason held his hand up to forestall the questions he knew were coming. "Natasha may have been right. We may be looking at something here that is sentient."

Amanda was shaking her head. "No way. Unless maybe

we've overlooked some stuff from the first two missions. Where we these things then?"

"Right. There's no evidence they found anything of this nature. Why us and why now?"

"Why not us?" Jason countered. "And maybe the things as you call them were asleep or hibernating. But it seems they knew exactly where to come to," he looked at Buzz, "Where did they other two missions touch down?"

Buzz didn't hesitate. "About two hundred clicks west of here. Both came down in the same valley. We can probably get Nat to confirm it, but I remember the strata was different. The boys back on Earth wanted to put us down in a sandy area so we could do more experiments. Now what do we do?"

He had asked the one question on everyone's mind. For long moments none of them said anything. Finally Harvey broke the silence. Jason jumped at the sound of his voice. Harvey had a resonance problem. He didn't know how to talk softly so he didn't talk much at all. "We haven't considered this might be an opportunity for first contact."

'Why didn't I think of that?' flashed through Jason's mind. "Because I felt the being's thoughts!" he said aloud. "That thing is nothing that we want to parley with. I felt it."

6 FIRST CONTACT

"When will it end?" Jason shouted but none of his crewmates answered. He glanced around the crew's quarters and realized they never would. Angela had put them in deep freeze awaiting re-entry into Moon Base approach. At that time the automatic docbots would kick in to rejuvenate the crew, or at least those who still had vital signs.

Tony and Marsella would never awake. Tears flowed from Jason's eyes as he remembered how hard she squeezed his hand; trying to hold onto life with all that was still in her. The anguish in her eyes told the story.

That they had to take off from Mars surface without completing seventy-five percent of the mission specifications was a blow to her morale. That they hadn't completed the life habitat her father had started on the first Mars mission was enough to cause her to become agitated. But that hadn't killed her. Jason walked over to her coffin and looked through the glass faceplate. The fungus was still growing.

'How did she become infected?' he asked for probably the ten thousandth time. He hurried to check the others. None of them showed signs of contamination. And what could he do if they were? He didn't have power left in the module to jettison them into space. He also had orders to bring them back into orbit prior to awakening anyone. Bernstein had been very specific about Colonel O'Keefe's orders.

Jason collapsed back into the command chair. His head slammed so hard into the headrest that he temporarily saw stars. A niggling thought eased its way through his mind as it cleared. 'Why am I sitting here by myself? Someone should be sitting up with me. It ain't fair I should be saddled with delivering these stiffs.'

A more chilling thought occurred to Jason. 'Why am I the only one left?' He leaned back into the headrest and considered the questions that were beginning to pour through a hole in his mind. Thinking felt good so he closed his eyes and tried to open the hole larger.

Time passed. Jason awoke with a start. He knew he had been asleep. 'Probably the first real sleep I've had in a long time,' he thought. He stretched his arms over his head and realized he felt refreshed. There had to be a valid explanation.

"There is."

Jason's head snapped around. Tony was sitting on the edge of his acceleration couch. His head was down, as if he were examining the deck beneath his feet.

Jason was astonished when Tony finally raised his face. It wasn't entirely human. Too white. The inside of Tony's mouth was too red when he opened it to speak. "Yes, Commander, I'm not exactly the Tony you remember. But don't worry about it."

Tony stood and approached. "You won't have to worry about much of anything soon." He turned back to the couch and sat down hard. "Man, these bodies are hard to get the hang of."

Jason felt as if he were frozen in place. His muscles didn't want to move. "There's a very good reason for that. We don't want you to move. You might get heroic and try to put this craft into some sort of self-destruct process. We can't have that, now can we?"

Tony seemed to arise effortlessly from the couch. "Its really amazing what a little rest will do for you. That and a little feeding." He pointed to Amanda's chamber. The top glass had been shoved back. Jason could just see enough of the chamber to know that she was still in it, but couldn't tell what her condition was.

"She's resting comfortably, now." Tony moved around to the next chamber in line and began pressing the sequence of buttons that would eventually open it. "I know, I've got to leave enough blood for the others. One can't get greedy until we get to your Moon Base, now can one?" He smiled maliciously as he walked back over and stood in front of Jason.

"The really ironic thing about this is that your blood will be tasted last. You see, we need you to be completely you or we may not make it back to Moon orbit at all." He placed his hands on his hips and studied Jason's face. "I want to see consternation finally dawn in your eyes as you realize the cargo you are delivering back to Earth, via the Moon, of course."

Jason found that he could speak again. "What are you and why are you doing this?"

Tony shrugged and went back to check the revitalization process that he had started. "About 20 percent completed. Too much nitrogen in his blood for it to be any good, but give it a couple hours…" Tony fell silent as he caught sight of the retreating ball that was his home planet.

"So that's what MarSome looks like from space. I've often wondered what my home would look like," he looked back at Jason, "you can't really appreciate what we are or how very long we've had to wait for you. Your race is so clumsy when compared to what we used to be."

Jason felt his muscles relax. Tony pointed to the command

chair and indicated that Jason was to sit. "Try to touch anything, Commander, and you'll be placed in rigid control again. It won't be pleasant, so let's keep this civil, shall we?"

Nodding as he sat Jason tried to clear all the thoughts that were coming fast. So many questions to be asked. It was obvious now that Amanda had been correct about this being first contact.

"Why us?"

"You mean, why were you chosen to carry us back to Earth instead of the first or second mission?"

"You obviously had time to prepare. Is that it?"

"Partially," Tony hesitated, and then continued. "You have to be aware of how long we have waited. The planet you call Mars was old when your people were planted upon the surface of your planet. Tens of thousands of your years have passed since my people viewed our world with physical eyes. Our two races could have co-existed, but your progenitors would have none of it. They wanted their experiment to be perfect."

Jason sat thinking about the implications of what he had just been told. "You are trying to tell me that we are not made in the image of our God?"

Tony's harsh laugh barked and echoed through a cabin that suddenly seemed to close for comfort. Jason shrank back into his couch and Tony continued. "Your people actually come from a planet that orbits a minor sun in the Deneb system. They come back from time to time to ensure the works of their hands are still viable."

"To what purpose?" Jason wanted to know.

"I don't have the answer to that question. We have never been made privy to the inner counsel of the Denebians. You see, there are some basic differences between our races. You noticed what you called fungus on your crewmember?"

Jason nodded. "Yeah, I noticed."

"You also wondered how we got through to her. A hole punched in the leg of her suit was easy to manage. You were right. You should not have sent anyone back out on the surface. We were terrified that you might have made that decision. That's why we tampered with her mind and made her so insistent to complete her father's work. Who, by the way, knew of our existence. You didn't know that, did you?"

"No. That wasn't in any of the debriefings from his mission. How did you accomplish that?"

"We merely convinced him that what he saw was delusional. He thought he was seeing what he called a mirage. What we showed him was how Mars used to look. He didn't see beneath the surface to discover our real natures."

Jason prompted after several moments of silence, "And that is?"

Tony's eyes widened as he considered the question. Where there should have been white around the pupils there was green. It made the dark brown of Tony's eyes even darker.

"We are basically a virus now. The green fungus you saw growing on your mate is the outer manifestation of the metabolizing process we must put your bodies through to co-exist with you. On your planet we drink your life's blood and you become transformed."

"You are a Vampire!" Jason exclaimed, aghast as the realization hit him that he had known all along. "The undead. I really didn't think you existed." He started to get up but Tony motioned for him to remain seated. Jason's lower body suddenly felt as if it were glued to his seat.

"You should have listened to your legends. Small parts of us were transmitted to your planet during a couple meteor storms that bombarded pieces off ours. We have been on your Earth for many centuries. We can't be killed by your people, only hindered in our quest to live quietly with you."

"But you feed on us." Jason was repulsed by the thought of something drinking his blood. Coldness grew in his stomach. He knew he had to do whatever it took to keep Earth from being infested. But first, he must find out more about the creature sitting across from him. He must know all he could about them.

"I agree with you, Commander," Tony smiled, "You do need to know everything about us. But as for getting a chance to do anything about the infestation of your planet, well, we can't allow that. You see, there will be enough of US by the time we reach your Moon that it won't matter what you do. There's already enough virus metabolized that we can actually crash land on your moon and still make our way into your biosphere."

He continued, "You were right about the first two missions. We weren't quite ready when the last one lifted off. Oh, we wanted to!" the excitement was evident as the creature within Tony remembered the patience required to accomplish its goal. "World domination is at our fingertips! Patience was a must."

Tony examined nails that had turned black and green. He held up his hand and seemed to notice for the first time the length of his claws. "With these sharpened to points, I could rip your beating heart from your still living body and drink the blood before the lights ever leave your eyes. Your kind is so fragile."

Jason shrank back as Tony licked his lips and bared his teeth. He noticed for the first time the two hollow fangs protruding from Tony's mouth. "Yes, they are painful. But necessary for us to feed on you. Imagine your wife and children offering their throats to me!"

Tony laughed gleefully as he looked deep into Jason's eyes. "That is a prospect that sends terror through your soul. Let me inform you right now, I intend to take your dear Molly to my bosom personally. You can count on that. I feel Tony's lust for her bursting out through my jeans!" Again he laughed deeply, enjoying the consternation on Jason's face.

"Now, sleep, little man. We are going to have much to do within a couple cycles to convince your people that we don't need their interference. Your Colonel O'Keefe is going to be a pain in the ass about this. But we have a surprise even for him."

He looked deep into Jason's soul and Jason felt his eyes grow heavy. Hours passed as Mars Mission III made its way back toward Earth.

7 MARSELLA AWAKENS

"Wake up, Commander. You've got work to do." Jason felt something brush against his face. His eyes didn't focus immediately and he wished they wouldn't after they did. Tony stood over him. His green eyes burned holes clear through him.

"Let me go back to sleep," he protested. "Maybe I can wake up and you won't be here." He brushed Tony aside and stood up. His bladder really needed to be emptied. "How long did you let me sleep?"

Tony shrugged and reached into Marsella's couch. Jason couldn't see what he was doing but he got the impression that the being was tenderly ministering to whoever lay there. He forgot about it as his bladder protested again. "Well, I'm going to relieve myself."

He looked back over his shoulder but it seemed Tony was ignoring him. His eyes scanned the command board on the way to the facilities. He couldn't remember how much time had passed but he did see that time since lift off from Mars surface was four months and nine days. They were exactly half of the way home. He contemplated that as he hooked up. SCAT came on line on the small monitor in front of him.

"Good Morning, Commander. Do You Want To Take Your Regular Battery Of Tests?" The cursor blinked on and off as he re-

read each word. His emotions seemed about to jump off the chart. Even a doctor in a box was better than talking with aliens. But he knew he had to control what he was feeling. He began typing on the little rubber keypad below the monitor.

"I need to talk with Moon Base Control. Can't explain now, but you are going to have to patch me through, bypassing the main computer console. This is a Direct Contact Order, serial 01 dash 549 dash omega 7."

Jason waited as SCAT processed his directive. He had finished with his ablutions, but stood there connected still. The suction was beginning to become a little painful so he flipped the switch to turn it off. He knew he dared not spend much time alone. Tony was sure to remember that there was a comms procedure built into SCAT. Then the shit would hit the fan.

"SCAT, when you have patched through, open up the main cabins comms channels and ensure constant monitoring from now on. Patch it through to Moon Base. Ensure they know this is a Direct Contact. Commander Martin out. Delta Fox Tango 4, 6, 19, Charlie." Jason watched the cursor blink for another moment before going back into the crew quarters.

Tony was helping Marsella stand. Her knees buckled and he bore her weight to his couch. She waved him away after she lay back. A deep, gravelly voice that definitely was not Marsella croaked, "Leave me alone. I'll survive if this body will cooperate. Funny there was no mention by our advanced scouts of any difficulty making these husks adjust to us." She turned her head and Marsella's body went through a coughing spasm.

Jason watched in fascinated horror as she went through a series of voice box adjustments until a voice came out that suited the creature. "Remind me to get even with you for saddling me with this body," she stated as she sat up. "Which one is ready?"

Tony motioned her to Buzz's console. "This one is ready. I tried to get him as close to ready as I could. His temperature was hard to regulate, but that shouldn't matter once you get finished with the fluid transfer," it seemed he was talking mainly for Jason's benefit.

Jason sat down as Marsella stumbled over and nearly fell onto her victim. He tried to shut his eyes, but he could not ignore the sounds she made, nor the sounds made by a semi-comatose Buzz. He groaned as she fed from wounds made above the artery in his neck. She had chosen to be rough because of the size of his neck.

"She probably is going to bust my chops because his blood won't suit her," Tony remarked, "Barsoom was always so finicky. He always wanted virgins. Dainty eater, that one."

"How can you be so callous?" Jason demanded.

"What, you mean, how can we feed on your body husks with such abandon?" Tony laughed, but there was no mirth in his voice. "Just wait until the last one wakes up. The way I figure it you have about three weeks before that happens. Who are you going to eat when you re-awaken, Commander?"

"What do you mean, who am I going to eat. No one! I'm not like you!" Jason was almost screaming. Marsella raised her head and looked at Tony. "Can't you shut him up? I'm trying to enjoy what I can of this radfish you've given me and you let him break my concentration. Really, Bartam. I thought you would be more agreeable after all this time."

Tony laughed again, this time there was happiness in it. "Shame that we have to be so open about the process, but you really have no privacy in these quarters. How did your people really think they could send you out in something so small?"

Jason looked around the crew quarters and for the first time felt the walls close in. "This is actually bigger than the other two missions."

"I know. We measured the dimensions carefully as you were landing. But everything came down to one thing. We couldn't take any more back than came."

"Huh?" Jason didn't have a clue what Tony was saying.

"Actually, Bartam was trying to tell you that we couldn't ship any more back to Earth than came from there to begin with," Marsella said as she stood and wiped the back of her hand across her mouth. Blood came away from her lips but she hungrily licked it into her mouth. Her smile was slightly sour as she considered the taste.

"That was not a good meal by any stretch of the imagination. I will repay you in kind some day," her eyes flashed as she made her way back to collapse on Tony's couch again. "Now be quiet while I rest."

Tony waved his hand in front of Jason's face. Jason felt nothing, but was instantly asleep. Tony sat and thought while time ticked off on the command console.

8 COMMUNICATIONS WITH MOON BASE CONTROL

"Well, Commander. You did well", Tony slapped Jason on the back after the communications channel had gone dead. He didn't seem to notice when Jason flinched away from his touch. Jason sat back and ran his fingers through his thinning hair. He thought it almost funny that he had never noticed how thin he was going on top. Now it probably wouldn't matter.

"You are so right," purred Marsella, stretching her lithe body in front of him. Jason hadn't quite gotten used to calling the creatures by their Martian names. Tony and Marsella sort of stuck in his mind, especially when he watched her trying to adjust to her new body. She slid up next to Tony and ran her fingers through his abundant hair, looking all the time at Jason.

"You surprised me, Commander," she stated with a lilt in her contralto voice. "I was ready for you to try and drop hints to your buddies about us." She moved closer until she was standing almost on top of him. He almost retched from the smell of blood that still clung to her clothes.

"Why didn't you try to warn them? I would have." Marcella looked back over at Tony. "If my body remembers everything from before I took over, shouldn't I have tried to warn them?"

Tony nodded. Jason didn't like the mean glint that came into Tony's eyes. Tony removed a razor blade from a storage compartment in his pants. "Why didn't you drop a hint?"

His eyes narrowed as he stepped toward Jason and motioned for Marsella to hold him. She grabbed a handful of thinning hair and twisted. Jason felt his neck strain as she lifted his head up and back. "I get half if you cut him," she said, but Tony only stood gazing at Jason.

"You know we can read your thoughts and I had a pretty tight grasp on them throughout the entire process. I didn't once think you were going to give us away. Why?"

Jason strained to say something. "We still have a long way to go. There will be other times and you might grow careless."

Tony crowed and twirled around on his heel. The razor ended up grazing Jason's throat as he completed his pirouette. "Don't get careless with me, Commander," he stated with no emotion at all in his voice. "My companions will like nothing better than to drain your worthless body and leave you in the corner someplace. There won't be any careless."

Marsella thrust Jason's head roughly toward his knees. Jason had to catch himself to keep from bumping into the side of the comms console. "Why don't we just go ahead?" she whined as Tony walked away.

He looked back over his shoulder. "Because we need him, remember? We are going to have five new members of our family any day now. They are going to require more than usual amounts of blood before they are truly ready to join us." He pointed at Jason and continued, "This one is going to wish we had left him behind before we finally kick his worthless body out an airlock".

Jason cringed away as Marsella wiped the spot of blood from his neck and tasted it. "They are going to like him," she said with a mixture of envy and relish in her voice. "We could do with one less, you know."

Tony turned on her fast. His hand surrounded her throat as he pushed her roughly against the bulkhead. "We have to have seven of us to control all the lay lines when we finally do get to Earth. And we don't want to be diluting the bloodlines any more than we have to. This original batch of virus has to last us until we can make our own trip back to open the crypts."

He patted her face and stepped back. "We need them. You sat in on enough of the planning sessions to know that." He looked up and down her body. "Don't let your new husk overwhelm your basic brain patterns."

Marsella hissed at him and ran her tongue over her lips. "I won't be warned by you," she stated with just a little mixture of fear and jealousy. "I was one of the original group, remember?"

Turning his back on her, Tony yawned. "It's about time for me to get some rest," he said as he surveyed all the hibernation chambers. "Wake me before this one is ready to come out", he patted Buzz's chamber. "I want to be here to help him adjust." He pointed a finger at Jason. "And keep that one in check. If he does anything, wake me." Tony thought about it for a moment, and then continued, "No, we need him to be asleep. I'll put him under and you better leave him alone."

Tony stood before Jason and established eye contact. It was too simple placing him into stasis. He turned back to Marsella. "You screw this up and I'll shove you out an airlock myself, got that?"

She continued to sulk long after Tony had laid down for his nap. There was nothing to do. "How do these creatures survive trips like these?" she asked, but no body answered. She looked around herself, desperate for something to do.

Nothing except Jason caught her eyes. Her body was starting to require things she had never thought about. She considered carefully. There might be ways to get what she wanted without violating Tony's orders. Maybe...

9 WORKING THE KINKS OUT

Marsella stood up and smoothed her skirt. Between her legs stretched the comatose body of Commander Martin. She stooped down and repositioned his outer coverings. 'You will please me even in your sleep, Commander,' she thought proudly to herself as she lifted his body into his command chair. 'No one has to know how you pleased me. That will be just between you and me. And you can't tell anyone.'

Stepping back, she ensured he was just as Tony had left him. She then turned on the ship's computer and spent the rest of Tony's rest cycle researching Earth culture. She was particularly pleased when she found a data base section entitled Folklore Around the Globe. Included in it were references to "her kind".

"Vampires are among some of the oldest denizens of the folklore tradition, dating back to prehistoric times…"

"No shit," she continued reading silently, commenting now and then over some of the more or less astute statements regarding her kind. "I wish we could do that," she said aloud when she read the passage on transmogrification. "Changing into a cat or some other creature is appealing."

"Yes, it is." Tony sat up as her head spun around. Marsella hissed and tried to back up. "You should warn someone before you intrude into their private conversations," she stated, trying to quell the alarm that had arisen in her stomach. 'How long has he been awake?' whispered within a private chamber within her mind.

Tony stood and surveyed the chambers. "Ah. Just in time." Without warning, he sprang on Marcella, pinning her against the bulkhead. His face was within inches of hers. "When were you going to wake me?" he growled and flung her across the room.

She landed heavily and propped herself on her arms as she tried to get her lower body to cooperate. It was out of alignment for some reason. She looked down and realized her lower torso was turned wrong. She knew there were a lot of coordination problems associated with a new body. Much more time was necessary to get everything to function correctly. Fierce anger at Tony coursed through her mind but she had to control it.

"You will go too far," she said as she lay back on the floor and turned her lower body over the right way. Cartilage and bones re-meshed and began to mend as she lay there. Silence flooded the compartment as they both waited. Tony for the timer to go off; Marsella for him to make a mistake.

The buzzer alarmed both when it went off finally. Tony jumped up and investigated the chamber. Within it, a body was beginning to stir. Popping the top, Tony secured the straps on Buzz's arms and upper torso. He didn't have to adjust for the lower extremities as they were still encased in the chamber.

Marsella finally stood and willed her legs to move in unison. She was shocked by the revulsion she felt looking over Tony's shoulder at the creature inside the chamber. Wild green tinged eyes stared back at her. Teeth champed within a wide mouth. Bloodlust caused the being's body to writhe in sheer pain and anguish.

"Get that thing under control before you release it," she said as she turned and walked out of the cabin. The last thing she wanted to see was it feeding. Hunger rose within her throat and she leaned against the bulkhead to steady herself.

She wanted to eat so badly. She was rocking back and forth, trying to get control of herself when she heard the hatch being closed between the two compartments. Tony stood on her side of the bulkhead and twisted the latch.

"Neither of us are strong enough to endure a feeding frenzy", was all he would say as he sat down beside her. "In a way I pity the Commander." Screams could be heard even through the insulation separating the compartments. Tony put his arm around Marsella's shoulders and pulled her near. She raised her lips to meet his. "Teach me how to use this body." She complied.

10 SCREAMING

Jason tried to raise his head. Something sticky covered his right eye. He could barely open the left one and it took several moments before he could get it to focus. It stung terribly. Blinking didn't do any good. Dried debris seemed to collect in it and he didn't have any way of digging it out. His head slumped forward. He hadn't the strength to raise it again for a long time.

Buzz, or more specifically, the creature that had grown out of Buzz, had done a job on him. Jason knew he had been thrown across the room at least three times before Buzz had him sufficiently softened up to begin feeding.

Tony and Marsella had disappeared right after Buzz's awakening. Jason hadn't wanted to take Tony seriously when he had talked about someone being food for the new vampires as they awoke.

He did now. He had paid the price for being complacent. Then he hadn't known what to expect. He and Buzz had been friends since college. Buzz wouldn't hurt him. However, the thing that inhabited his body would. It had been particularly nasty in its feeding habits. Jason looked down the length of his body and noticed his pants were around his ankles. Buzz hadn't bothered to pull them back up afterwards.

Buzz had forced Jason onto his stomach, ripped his pants down, and didn't begin feeding until he had entered Jason's body. Jason almost screamed again as the pain filtered back into his body. But he couldn't. He didn't have the strength. He barely had the presence of mind to realize others were in the compartment again.

Tony placed his hand on Buzz's shoulder. "Welcome to the new world", he said as he checked Angela's chamber. "She's almost ready." He looked over at Jason. "You did leave enough inside that one to feed one more, didn't you?"

Buzz nodded and turned away. He couldn't believe what he had done. Bloodlust was still in control of him as he turned back. "I want the husk for myself. I need to use it again."

"Well, you won't be able to", Marsella pointed out when Tony didn't respond. "We have to share, so you're going to have to concentrate on something else." She cupped Buzz's chin in her hand but he pulled away from her sharply.

"Don't try anything on me," he hissed. "I may still be weak but I'm no fool. The plan was to use the crew until we could get into their moon's compound. How much time do we have until that takes place?" He looked at Tony.

"Another three months, at the least. Unless we can get one of their ships to come to us. Marsella and I are working on that angle."

They all fell silent for some time. However, they all felt something beginning to settle in on them. Buzz finally spoke the thought that was weighing on all of them. "Boredom. How are we going to cope with the boredom?"

Marsella looked from one man to the other. "I don't know about you, but I could do with a little more practice." She flexed her arms over her head and tried to gaze seductively at Buzz.

Tony's backhand caught her in mid-stride. She wiped her

mouth with the back of her own hand and prepared to jump him. Buzz stepped between them. "You two lovers are going to have to jet back."

Tony pointed around Buzz at Marsella. "You had better learn how to control yourself", was all he said, but she read volumes in his eyes. She knew jealousy when she saw it. After one session, Tony already considered her his property. 'I will show him,' she thought silently.

They broke away from each other as a cry came from the chamber of the newly awakened. Tony pressed the buttons to release her and then herded them all into the next compartment. He looked back at the Commander and almost felt pity for him. The next couple hours were not going to be good for him.

He shrugged as Jason tried to lift his head and make eye contact. He saw horror dawn in the Commander's good eye as he shut the hatch. He also saw the creature Angela had become creeping out of its chamber, looking for blood.

Jason screamed.

11 SPRUNG TRAP

"How close are they?" Angela looked back over her shoulder at their new commander. Tony had automatically assumed that role since he was the first one to re-create himself in human form. She wasn't committed to his leadership. She had been number two under Commander Martin, but he was in no condition to command anything. She glanced over at the emaciated body lying under the comms cabinet. He hadn't moved in some time.

"I asked you for distance from the target." Tony shouted so loud that Angela jumped. "Get your mind on what you're doing," he growled as they made eye contact.

"Approximately twenty miles and closing."

"Good," Tony glanced over at Buzz. "They still don't suspect a thing", was the reply he got.

"Good, good. We can use a break. You guys realize this is going to be the first battle in space conducted in nearly twelve thousand years?" Tony's eyes narrowed as he looked through the observation port at their rescuers. He and Marsella had put out a call for rescue right after they had taken over. Now almost six months had passed and they were finally going to get what they wanted.

Angela broke in on his train of thought. "We need to turn on the outside navigation beacons for them. They have their radars painting us now but will still need the beacon to dock with us."

Tony reached over his shoulder and flipped several switches. "Satisfied?"

Angela retracted her head into her shoulders and bit her tongue. There was no way that that insufferable bastard was going to remain mission commander beyond the Moon base. She was determined to get together with the others to ensure that. She looked out the corner of her eyes at him and realized he was already feeling the bloodlust of having new victims so near. Buzz noticed it also.

"Control yourself, Commander," he cautioned softly.

With less than ten miles between the intervening spacecraft, everyone got down to the business of docking. Twenty minutes passed swiftly as minds concentrated on bringing their vectors and velocity into sync. Everyone in Mars Mission III jumped when the airlocks touched and a new voice came through the umbilical connection between them.

"Mars Mission III, this is Commander Silkmani from Moon Base Rescue. Open your inner hatch so we can board, please. And let me be the first to welcome you back to the land of the living."

Tony verbalized under his breath, "Yeah, this is going to be the land of the living", but he acknowledged their rescuers. "Thank you, Commander Silkmani. We are sure glad to hear your voice. Our communications have been out for so long. Opening the hatch now."

The hatch opened and Tony stood to welcome the first arrivals from the other craft. Two marines stepped through with stun guns leveled. Marsella tried to make a pre-emptive jump on one of them, but the third coming through the hatch unloaded on her. Her body reacted as a couple thousand volts of electricity stormed through the metal dart that impacted her chest. She slumped and fell heavily to the floor.

The others were mesmerized by the sudden turn of events. Tony held his hands up in front of him and signaled surrender. "That's a good decision," the nearest marine stated. "Now, get down. Flat on the floor. Place your hands palm up stretched out in front of you. Move!"

Tony followed the others to the deck. Cuffs were placed on his left wrist and his arm was twisted into his back. The marine placed his knee between Tony's shoulder blades and pressed down. Air whooshed from his lungs. He heard the same from the others as they were also trussed up. The marines finally stood up after attaching the neck ring to the ankle chains.

"We're all secure here, Commander. Only had one of them try to be a hero."

"Are they all conscious?" Commander Silkmani inquired.

"Yes, all but the one we blasted. She's starting to show life again. These creatures must have iron constitutions."

"Yes, and that's why you are going to be very careful with them. Place the explosive components into their collars and let me know when they can be armed."

The marines complied with orders, then placed explosive charges on each of the sleep chambers. Finally, they stood back to survey their work. "Captain, secure the craft and return to your station."

"Roger, sir."

The three marines moved as one, exiting the spacecraft and securing the hatch behind them. Tony craned his neck to look up at it after it sealed. Above the hatch, a new box had been pasted to the bulkhead. Three camera lenses stuck out of it.

"People, we've been had," Buzz grunted from where he lay. No one spoke for a long time until Marsella started shaking her head and struggled with her restraints. Angela sent her a tight-beamed thought. 'Don't you dare break those chains. You hear me?'

Marsella nodded finally and seemed to subside. On the other ship, a celebration was taking place as Commander Silkmani passed out the cigars. "You gentlemen can't light them till we get back to Moon Base, but that doesn't mean they can't be chewed on. Good work." He turned to the communications board and flipped the switch that opened channels directly to Colonel O'Keefe's office.

"We have them, sir. They didn't even know what hit them. Had to drop one of them in her dainty little tracks, but they are all trussed up good now."

O'Keefe grunted and slid his feet off his desk. "Don't make any mistakes with them, Commander. We can't let these things get to Earth."

Space and distance crackled over his office speaker as he waited for Silkmani to respond. Minutes went by. Finally, Silkmani asked the question O'Keefe was ready for. "Did you want us to go back for Commander Martin?"

"Can you see him in the camera?"

"Barely. The angle isn't that good, but we can just make out his legs and lower back."

"Is he moving, man? Can you see anything that would indicate he is still alive? The only way we break that hatch open again short of entry into Moon orbit is if you see something that indicates he is alive."

"We will monitor the situation, sir."

O'Keefe sat back and switched off the speaker. His eyes tried to focus on the paper in front of him, but tears filmed his eyes. He dragged his hands across his eyes and tried to clear them. He had known Jason Martin his entire life.

Jason's father had taught him how to fly. Had been one of the best test pilots in the business. Now Jason was either dead or near death, if he could believe the transmission Moon Base had received from the Commander. He picked it up, along with the translation. Commander Martin had somehow contrived to use the comm pad in the urinal to send a message.

This is a message from Jason Carpenter. Mars Mission III has been high jacked!

Vampires have taken over the crew by converting us into their kind. The mission must be stopped at all cost prior to entry into Earth's orbit.

These creatures are virus based. There already are some of their kind on our planet. Research existing records for vampires.

Gentlemen, they are real!

Carpenter out

O'Keefe read the short message again and again. He had probably gone over it now so many times he could repeat it in his sleep. That Martin had been able to get it off at all was a miracle. That he had pointed them in the right direction had helped immensely.

Jason had also proven why he had been chosen for this mission. The fact that he had used Carpenter as his last name instead of Martin was pre-planned. During mission workup, they had inserted that precaution into Jason's training. Carpenter meant they were to take seriously everything said in the message.

"Ain't never seen a vampire," the Colonel muttered. "I think I'd consigned myself to never seeing one, but now the cat's out of the bag."

He glanced over at the massive book his secretary had brought in and placed upon his desk. INSTRUCTIONS FOR ALIEN CONTACT was stamped in red letters over the face of the binding. He sighed and settled in for a long evening. Everyone from the President on down to cabinet members was listed in the preliminary pages. He had some calls to make.

Meanwhile, everyone aboard the Pegasus was glued to the monitors, trying to get some indication that Commander Martin was alive.

12 HE'S THE ONE

"He's the one."

Molly looked up suddenly from the book she was reading. Her eyes focused on the old woman standing in front of her. Her mind still hadn't caught up. She frowned and laid her book spine up on the table. She usually chose Back Yard Burger because she could sit quietly and read after finishing her lunch. What had the woman said? She couldn't remember.

"He is the one," the woman repeated. She was clutching an old, frayed, black purse tightly to her abdomen. Molly looked toward the door and noticed that three middle aged people appeared to be waiting for the woman.

"Do I know you?" she asked. The lady screwed up her face and replied, "No, sweetie. You don't. But I know he's the one."

Molly felt her exasperation level starting to max. "Who are you talking about?" Her voice was a little louder than she wanted and must have been louder than the woman desired. She held her hands out in front of her as if trying to get Molly to keep her voice down.

"Your husband is on his way back from Mars. They should never have let him go." She shut up as one of the men who had been waiting approached the table. "Come on. We need to be going."

He looked at Molly sympathetically, "She hasn't bothered you, has she?" He continued as Molly shook her head, "We have a hard time taking her out in public. She thinks she sees things. I apologize for her upsetting you."

They moved off toward the door with Molly staring after them. The old lady looked back at her as the door closed. The look in her dark eyes spoke volumes. Molly started to get up to follow them, but the woman shook her head. For some reason Molly knew she would see her again.

Minutes passed as she considered the incident. What had the woman been talking about? She obviously knew her because she had said something about Jason returning from Mars. She hadn't mentioned him by name. Molly felt a cold spot growing in the pit of her stomach as she remembered something else the woman had said. "They should never have let him go."

'What does she know?' Molly thought long and hard, but could come up with nothing. She had been briefed with the other family members when the mission lifted off Mars prematurely. They were told that everything was fine, but due to two casualties had decided to return early.

Molly had thought during the briefing that that explanation was just a little too pat. Jason would have stayed on planet even if half his crew were gone. She was now convinced of that now and probably should have been during the briefing.

"They are hiding something," she stated flatly. She wished again that she could call O'Keefe. The Colonel wouldn't lie to her. She knew that for a fact. She would stake her life on him being straight with her.

He had kind of taken her under his wing when Jason had joined NASA. She had always thought it was because of her resemblance to his deceased daughter. It was uncanny how much she looked like Tanya. It was also unreal how close they had become. He was the only man, other than Jason, who she allowed to touch her. He would always put his arm around her shoulder and hug her.

"I could really use that arm now," she muttered as she marked the place in her book and placed it into her shopping bag. It was about time to go pick up the kids from her mothers. They had a standing appointment on Fridays. She took the kids to her mom's and went shopping. Just herself. It was the only time during the week when she had time to herself. All other time was taken with work and the kids.

She considered what to do to find some answers as she drove the kids home. Thoughts were still going through her head as the kids got their bath. There really was no one at NASA that she could call. She finally picked up the phone and called Nancy Keith. Nancy and Harvey were divorced but Molly thought she might have kept in touch with how things were going with the mission.

The phone rang six times before a sleepy voice answered. "This is Nancy and this better be good."

Molly apologized for disturbing her. "Nancy, this is Jason Martin's wife. You do remember me from the pre-flight briefings, don't you?"

Nancy instantly sounded more alert. "Of course I do. Has someone heard something from the guys?"

"No. At least not since the briefing they had when the mission lifted off", she got interrupted as Nancy sat bolt upright in bed. "Would you repeat that? They have lifted off? I thought Harvey said they would be there for another two years. What happened?"

"I don't know. NASA's PR people said Jason had decided to lift off early because of two casualties that the mission suffered. They wouldn't say who or what happened", she halted as she heard a sob coming from the other side of the phone.

"I'm sorry, Nancy. I thought you and Harvey were divorced." Her voice trailed off.

Molly waited for several moments while Nancy collected her thoughts. "There was no way you could have known. Harvey wanted us to split before the mission but then contacted me a week before they left and asked me to wait for him. They didn't say who the casualties were?"

"No. And no one else had family besides us. I don't know what to think."

"Me neither. I guess they didn't think about contacting me because of us being divorced. Well, I'm going to set some PR people straight first thing in the morning. Thanks, Molly." There was a pause, then she continued, "But you didn't call for that, did you?"

Molly had to admit to herself that that wasn't why she had called. "Nancy, I have to talk with someone and you were the only person I could think of."

"Something has you spooked, hasn't it?" Nancy inquired.

"Yes, something happened to me today that really has me scared." She paused and then launched into a description of the day's events. Nancy remained silent and allowed her to finish.

"I can see why you would get spooked. And you don't know or didn't recognize the old woman?"

"I'm positive I would know her if I had ever seen her before," Molly avowed. "She seemed to be someone who is kept under lock and key in an old folk's home. The guy was really sorry that she had bothered me. Do you think she knows something that we haven't been told?"

"I can't think how. How did she know that you are Jason's wife?"

"I don't know. And that's starting to scare me more than her statements."

Nancy agreed. "Listen, honey. You want to come and stay with me until we get some answers? This house is huge and I have a big back yard where the kids can play."

"Sounds good, but I can't take time off right now and I kind of look in after my mother since she is alone now that Dad passed away. I appreciate the offer, but I just needed someone to talk with about the incident. I'll be fine."

"Well, call me if you change your mind. And I wouldn't worry too much, about what an old woman had to say. She probably saw your picture with Jason in a magazine and couldn't resist winding you up. The look on your face probably made her day. Don't you think?"

"Yeah, you're probably right. Thanks for listening. I'll let you know when I hear anything."

"Thanks, bye."

Molly sat holding the phone for a long time after Nancy hung up. Something was still bothering her. Nancy's analysis just seemed to good to be true. Suppose the woman was right and the crew never should have been sent – what then? Was the old woman trying to warn her or scare her?

"I don't care which she was going for – scared she certainly accomplished," she stated as she hung the phone back up. Something was going on and she was determined to find out what. She looked at the bed and shrank back into her chair.

It suddenly looked too big for just her. She finally got up and went to the children's room. A large, overstuffed chair looked out of their window at the field behind the house. Molly pulled a quilt around her, settled into the chair, and laid her head against the back of the chair. The moon was now approaching full so white light filtered in through the curtains. She finally drifted off to sleep.

13 CONVERSATION BEING UNEQUAL

Tony craned his neck around so he could see Buzz. Line of sight always helped with silent communications and he preferred to look into a person's eyes when they talked. 'Has Ailea gotten in touch with the woman?'

Buzz opened his eyes and brought his concentration back to the here and now. 'Yes, she made contact earlier today. Says she absolutely spooked the woman. I would like to have been there for that. Just a minute.' Buzz closed his eyes for a couple moments to concentrate on the reception. Tony couldn't do anything but wait.

Buzz finally signed off and sighed. 'Earth looks so good through her eyes.'

'Enough!' Tony shouted across the short distance between them. 'We don't have time for any of that stuff. Has she planted the bug on Martin's wife or not?'

'Not. And don't be too hasty. She has to be isolated before they can do anything with her. You of all people know how finicky these Earth people are about allowing total strangers to access their bodies.'

Tony relaxed as much as the restraints would allow. 'Yeah, I know. Well, keep me up to date on what happens with her. We need her to shake things up for us.' He scrunched up his shoulders to try and work some kinks out of his aching muscles. It didn't help much.

Angela joined their conversation. 'When are we going to go to work on our captors?'

'Shortly. Very shortly, in fact.' Tony cleared his throat and tried to project his voice. At first, he could only get out a couple croaks as the restraint around his neck was choking him. He finally got enough play in the metal cord and addressed the comms speaker on the desk across from him.

"Can anyone hear me? Do you have the comms channel open?" He waited and then repeated the questions. After about six times the voice of Commander Silkmani answered, "Yes, we hear you. What do you want?"

"Thank God, Commander. For a moment there I thought the comm. link was dead between us."

"I don't have time for idle chit chat", the Commander interrupted rudely, "Get down to what you want".

"Of course. For starters, we need to be released from these restraints. My kidneys are about to bust."

Again, the Commander stepped on Tony's side of the conversation. "You don't have kidneys as a true human being would have them. We know that. Our scanners have been busy and the lab boys back at Moon Base are really wanting to get their hands on you. Don't think they've ever seen anything as bizarre. So what do you really want?"

"Ok, Commander. We want freedom of movement over here. You can leave the explosives rigged but we want to be able to move around."

"That is not going to happen. I have personal orders to keep you trussed up just as you are. We don't want any funny stuff taking place."

"You mean like us taking over the ship and crashing into Earth, etcetera, etcetera?"

"Yes, something like that." Both men seemed to pause and time dragged out into minutes.

"We will go absolutely stir crazy without something to occupy our time. This isn't the kind of treatment you would get if you came to our planet."

"No, you just stick a claw into our crewmembers and infect the Hell out of them. Is that your idea of civility?"

Tony grimaced. "Ouch, Commander. You clearly got me there. What arrangements can we make? We are clearly here now and it must already be obvious that we aren't going anywhere. If you weren't interested, you would have turned this tub around and deposited us back into the landscape from whence we came. So what gives?"

"You're right. We have been interested since Mission I. We knew someone was there after the mission returned."

"So you sent more people to tempt us to hitch a ride?"

"Roger that. We were surprised when you didn't bite on the second mission. Me and my boys were ready for you that time."

Silence lengthened as Tony considers how much to say. Finally, "Yeah, well we had to consider the logistics of getting our people off planet. You NASA people know all about that, now don't you?"

"As a matter of fact, we do. Listen, I suggest you settle in and endure the ride. We have at least three weeks before we enter moon orbit and I don't think you're going to be too inconvenienced prior to our getting there. The bottom line is that we have orders to bring you in. Your condition was expressly specified in those orders. Restrained. Colonel O'Keefe said you could be dead and restrained and he would be pleased. So restrained you shall stay. Silkmani out."

Tony relaxed as best he could and turned his thoughts to the others. 'We have to find a way to make him see it our way before we get to the Moon.'

No one said much for a while, then Angela put out a thought, 'Why can't we just wait until we get there? Surely something can be passed during disembarkation.'

Buzz answered her. 'You saw the force fields they had around the hatch of their spacecraft. You also should know how much power we had to use to overcome their defenses. Moon Base is not going to just open up and let us waltz in there. They will take us to the most secure place they've got. And they've had time to work on it.'

Marsella piped into the conversation finally. 'I know where. They will take us to the demarcation facility Dad was working on. It's so far from anywhere that we would be worse than isolated. It's on the dark side. I hate the dark.'

'The bad news is that so do most humans,' Buzz quipped, 'we are going to become more human as we go through this. They could conceivably leave us in the dark for a long time. I would if I were in their situation.'

'Me, too,' Tony admitted. 'We must get something done before we arrive, so I suggest we all concentrate on our assigned tasks.'

'But I don't have a task,' Marsella whined.

'You do now. I need you to connect with your father and see if you can dredge anything out of the old man's brain that could help us.'

Tony turned his attention to Buzz and Angela. 'Is there any way that we can shut down the propulsion systems and make someone come out to pick us up?'

'I've been thinking about that,' admitted Buzz, 'we can be almost positive that they will detonate the device at the first hint that we've been able to tamper with any of their systems. That is probably not an option.'

'I can mentally encapsulate the device, but the energy is going to have to go somewhere and we don't have time to devise everything we need,' Angela's voice trailed off as she settled in to think about the situation.

Tony had to admit he didn't have any good ideas of his own. Buzz and Angela were probably right. He nudged Buzz mentally. 'Let me know when Ailea has something for us.'

14 RESCUE

Sgt Brinkley suddenly sat upright and yelled for Commander Silkmani, "He moved!" Silkmani dropped the paperback he had been trying unsuccessfully to read. His head swung round to concentrate on the monitor before his feet even hit the floor.

"Are you sure? We have to make sure it was Commander Martin moving and not one of them monsters trying to fool with our heads." They waited as time hacks clicked by on the screen in front of them. Everyone on the Pegasus was crowded around. The air was electric as they all but willed him to move again. "The only way I can justify opening that airlock again is to rescue him."

He was startled as Sgt Brinkley pointed at the monitor and shouted, "See, right there. He moved his legs. See, they are straighter than they were a moment ago."

"Replay the tape and let's see what we can pick up", Silkmani instructed, but he realized as soon as he said it that they didn't have to. Commander Martin was levering his upper torso off the deck and trying to look around him. He managed to get one arm to lock into place but the other wouldn't support him so he collapsed and rolled over.

"We have our mandate. Everyone get into riot gear. We are

going over there loaded for everything that can happen. I want no one to get between any other team member and those beings. Curtis, Chavez, and Butler, you're with me. Brinkley, I want you to closely monitor our friends and tell me the instant one of them moves."

"Are we going to let them know we're coming or just barge in?" Chavez wanted to know as he stepped into the lead lined boots all of them were now wearing.

The Commander paused for a moment. "No, I think we surprise them."

On the other ship, there was no surprise. Angela had been the first to come to alert as she had monitoring duty. 'Something has happened over there,' she thought to the others. 'They're all centered around the monitor station. Wonder what spooked them?'

Buzz answered the question. 'Look at our friend.' They all turned their attention to Commander Martin as he tried to lift himself up and then rolled over. 'They've been monitoring us to see if the Commander was still alive. Probably didn't think to check him when they bolted out of here the first time.'

Tony found this news to be amusing. 'Here's an angle we hadn't considered. Angela, I thought you used up the last drop of blood in that husk. What went wrong?'

'Don't blame me,' she almost screamed, 'he was bone dry when I finished with him. He can't possibly have anything else inside him.'

'Well, he does. It's almost as if he incubated and is now one of us. Buzz, scan his body completely. We might be delivering the package we need right into their laps.'

While Buzz was making his scans, Angela kept them apprised of the movements aboard the Pegasus. 'They're in their full riot gear now and appear to be ready to winch us into loading position.' They could all hear the strain on the outer hull as the cable tightened and began inching the two spacecraft closer. A dull thump let them know that someone had boarded from the Pegasus. Minutes passed as they waited.

'You were right, boss,' Buzz stated flatly just before the hatch opened. 'He has enough of our virus in his body to infect half the planet. Appears we might have our way in.'

The armed figure who entered first quickly went to the back of the cabin and held his weapon in readiness. "This is Curtis. The field of fire has been established. We can now secure the body."

"Roger that," Brinkley replied and relayed the message. Chavez and Butler quickly covered the distance between the hatch and Commander Martin's location. It took both of them several minutes to get him into his space suit. He was then lifted onto a stretcher and Butler backed out of the hatch. They had to stand the stretcher upright in the cycling station.

Curtis waited patiently until the hatch reopened and then scampered across the distance. He ensured the explosive device above the hatch was once more armed, and then closed it behind him.

'That went fairly smooth,' commented Buzz. 'Think they have any way of knowing that he is one of us?'

'I don't know. But, we are going to find out. Right, Angela?' Tony directed a dirty cloud of thought toward Mars III's former medical officer. 'Do you think they have the gear that will detect the virus?'

'I don't see any on board their ship. If they had thought to use the stasis beds over here, they could have made that determination, but I see nothing there. Especially if they leave him inside his suit. Their commander is on the comms link with Moon Base reporting that he is alive.'

'Well, continue monitoring them.' Tony was silent for several minutes, and then turned his attention to the one person who had been quiet during the entire episode. 'Marsella,' he quipped, 'tell us how the Commander came to have enough virus in his body to incubate a serum to replace his blood,' he focused on Angela for a moment, 'wouldn't you say that's what happened, doctor?'

Angela mentally nodded. 'Yes, I think that is a very close analysis of what happened,' she agreed. 'I've been trying to piece it together myself and that is the only reasonable explanation for why he is still alive.'

Attention turned back to Marsella. 'So what did happen while I was sleeping?'

Marsella stammered for a moment as Tony's essence pressed her into herself. 'I just had some fun with him. He was never awake. I just took advantage of what came up naturally.' She felt her face and neck warm with embarrassment.

'You couldn't control your animal instincts for more than a moment!' Tony drilled into her viciously. 'Now we are faced with an uncontrollable situation. We don't know how he is going to react when he finally realizes what we did to him.'

Buzz stepped into the conversation. 'We probably aren't in as much difficulty as we think. He can't turn himself in before they make docking. Silkmani would either throw him out the airlock or send him back over here with us. Personally, I think he will be quiet until they get to the Moon. After that,' he mentally shrugged, 'all bets are off.'

'It's the after that that scares me,' Tony admitted, then continued, 'we must try to establish communications with him before we get there. Angela, do you think he might be ready for that?'

She considered. 'I don't think so. I can't find anything more than REMs in his brain waves at this time. I suggest we wait until he has awakened at least once.'

'I agree,' Tony turned his attention back to Marsella. 'You ever cross me again and I'll personally cut your body up and feed you through a grinder.'

15 ON THE DARK SIDE OF THE MOON

Sgt Brinkley relayed the message from Moon Base Control to Commander Silkmani, "They're putting us into synchronous orbit for deposit of cargo at Moon Base Ten. I've passed the coordinates to Curtis already."

Commander Silkmani looked up from his position in the co-pilot's chair. The frown on his face said he already knew where they were taking their cargo. He had been through the facility before they blasted off on their present mission. He wasn't sure it could adequately contain those they were going to deposit there. But Command Staff had determined that it was the best place to provide containment.

"Very well," he said, turning to Captain Curtis, "Let me know when we get there."

"Roger, sir." Everything was quiet for several minutes. Only the clicks from their open comms line with the other ship provided an intruding background. "Pardon me, sir. How are we going to land the Mars Lander? I assume one of us will have to take it down."

"Yes. We can't land it by autopilot. They were never configured for that. Two of you will have to provide cover while you take it in."

Across the vacuum between the two ships, mental ears were listening intently. 'We might just get a break,' Buzz thought to his compatriots.

'Yes, if we take them out after touchdown. Angela, do you have any news about your containment field for their explosives device?' Tony demanded.

'Just give me a couple more minutes, then I can answer that.' Her thought patterns were concentrated on the task at hand so she didn't give any of them much consideration.

Marsella insinuated herself into Angela's thoughts. 'I've been following what you're doing. Maybe I can assist you.'

Angela accepted the offer, mostly because she knew that Marsella was going to need to get herself back into the category of being useful. Who knew what alliances would have to be drawn from in the days to come?

Tony and Buzz were concentrating on overpowering the crew of the Pegasus. 'We let them do the touchdown, then close down their minds. I think that will work,' Buzz was saying.

'Yes, but we have to ensure the Pegasus is also touched down before we act on anything. If it stays in orbit we might have a problem,' Tony countered.

'Not really. We still need at least three bodies so we can awaken the others. Silkmani is going to give us that many. What I'm really concerned about is not the Pegasus so much as any other ships they may be able to deploy, or already have deployed. Man, I'd have a couple cruisers in orbit to ensure we don't make a break for it. You aren't thinking we can withstand their nuke arsenal, are you?'

'I wouldn't be so stupid. We don't want to come anywhere near radioactivity. The signature would impregnate us indelibly for about ten thousand years. We would never have any peace on Earth. It would be like appearing on someone's doorstep with a sign on our backs saying 'track us'. No we can't allow that. Have you scanned any of their ships in the area?'

'Negative. And that puzzles me. How about at the facility?'

'No thought processes there,' Tony admitted he was clearly baffled by that, 'Have we underestimated these people?'

'That seems to be obvious, doesn't it?' Buzz countered, 'We are trussed up like their holiday turkeys, are we not?'

'Point taken. And we thought we were going to just sail smoothly into their Moon and quietly take over. I'm still wondering what happened,' his voice trailed off as he looked over at Marsella.

Angela broke in on their musings. 'I have it. Would never have done it without Marsella's help.'

'You're certain you can contain the explosion?' Tony demanded.

'Yes, certain. We merely project it into space. Redirect the energies. We don't have to worry about that.'

'Very well, ola, looks like they're getting ready to board us again. Now's the decision time. We have to all agree on this course of action. What do we do?'

Buzz cast his vote for caution. Angela cast hers also for caution. Marsella was silent. Tony cast his for taking the crew only if they could get the Pegasus to touch down. He turned to Marsella, 'Well, you are still a member of the group. What do you suggest?'

'I think we need to be cautious. Isn't it possible that we could allow them to pick up their crew and go on to Moon Base, then find a way to make our way there ourselves? We don't yet know what kind of equipment we might find at this base.'

'Good point,' Buzz answered for the rest of them. He was still not convinced that they had seen all of Earth's resources. 'Let's see what surprises they might have cooked up for us. I think its possible we can turn the tables on them.'

They were still debating the issues when the Pegasus crew boarded once more. They were taking no chances. Something else hadn't been counted on. Chavez pointed a new weapon at the aliens and depressed the stud.

Cold, intense, and debilitating swept over the floor of the Lander. Four beings screamed in unison as their bodily functions were frozen. Consciousness blacked out almost immediately.

Many hours of missing time passed before Marsella finally came back to her senses. Her body was strapped to a metal table. She could barely use her peripheral vision to see that the others were secured in a similar fashion. Black spots appeared in her field of vision as she tried to see if any of them were awake. Her mind finally succumbed to the mind numbing silence of the facilities and she passed out again.

Angela was awake when Marsella came back to herself. 'I was beginning to think the rest of you were permanently mal-functioning,' she said in relief as Marsella tried to move her head.

Marsella considered the others for a few moments. 'Don't worry. Our men will be awake shortly. But before they do I have a favor to ask of you. I also have to thank you for sticking your neck out for me back there. You didn't have to do that.'

'I know I didn't, but you didn't deserve the trashing that Tony has given you. I might have done the same thing if I'd been awakened first. What is the favor?'

'I have a feeling I'm going to need an ally during the coming months. I'd like to think I can count on you?'

Angela considered for a few moments, then answered, 'Of course. I know how over bearing Tony can be. Just don't give him issue, ok?'

'Ok. Now how are we going to get out of here?'

'I've been giving it some thought. They have thought of quite a lot in making this our final resting place. There are several circuits that we're going to have to circumvent before even one of us can touch the floor. And even that appears to be electrified. We need the guys to wake up so we can conference on this one.'

They both settled back to consider their prison.

16 QUARANTINE

Jason felt as if his head was going to explode. A couple aspirin would do him a world of good, he thought. He raised his head and looked around the sterilized room.

Doctors had poked and prodded him since the Pegasus crew had brought him in. And they had found nothing. Now he was going through standard quarantine.

'I wish they would let me out of here,' he stated for perhaps the thousandth time. 'There is nothing wrong with me.' He allowed himself to lie back and tried to relax. Patience would have to be sought after to get through this part of the ordeal. That was to be expected. And Moon Base staff were expected to be thorough in conducting their tests and all the associated paperwork.

A red light came on the comm. terminal across the room. Jason sat up and spoke into the mike in his sleeve to acknowledge. "Commander Martin, are you up to receiving a visitor on line?"

"Roger. Patch them through."

The visual signal resolved itself to show Colonel O'Keefe sitting behind his desk. "Jason, you look like crap warmed over," O'Keefe began, "are you sure they brought back to correct astronaut on that rescue mission?'

He chuckled, then continued, "I am glad to see you made it back, son. Molly has been tearing the trees down trying to find out how you are."

"How is she?" Jason asked.

"She's doing reasonably well. Some nut got to her and upset things about a month ago. We tried to assure her that everything was alright but she seemed to know before we did that you were on your way home."

Jason swallowed hard. His throat felt constricted as he thought of what she must have been going through. "Well, sir, family always was the downside to going into space. We knew that when we joined up."

"I know you did, son." O'Keefe paused for a moment. "I'm terribly sorry about your crew. We couldn't save any of them."

"Where are they now?" Jason ventured, then saw the clouds roll across the Colonel's face.

"You don't need to know," was all O'Keefe would say.

"How many of them hatched?" Jason tried to change his approach.

"Four. As far as we can tell all the others are still inside the stasis consoles onboard your craft. We have all of them contained where they can't escape. That's all you need to know about that at this point. Tell me about their plans. Did they discuss anything with you? I think they were surprised you made it back."

Jason knew a leading statement when he heard it. Frankly, he was surprised he had made it back. He remembered the black spots floating before his eyes as Angela had her way with him. He couldn't have had much left in his system.

He shook his head. "Yeah, they discussed their plans. No reason not to. Tony, or whoever it is who is now in Tony's body, was adamant that I should know what they were going to do."

O'Keefe settled back in his chair. "Tell me as much as you can recall. We're going to have the psych boys put you through the normal hypnotic debrief tomorrow, but I want a chance to think about what they might have told you."

"Well, chief, there might be holes in my remembering, but they were intent on getting to Earth via the Moon. Apparently they couldn't agree on how many they needed to make their conquest viable. I heard one comment about them needing seven."

"Did they say why?"

"Not in so many words. Something about ley lines was associated with that number."

Both men were quiet for a moment. O'Keefe finally looked away from the terminal where he had been looking up some information.

"Well, there are seven ley lines that intersect the Earth. It is postulated by our scientists that they could be used for energy transfer. We don't know how. Frankly, we don't know much about their methods of getting around on Mars. Did they give a clue about that?"

"Negative. I learned very little about their habits on Mars. Tony told me about how Mars used to have an atmosphere and oceans and all that. He mentioned having prime beach front property before the disasters struck."

"What kind of disasters? Did he say?"

"No. Only that the Denebians had something to do with them."

"Who are the Denebians?" O'Keefe sat forward in his chair and stared into the screen. Jason definitely had his attention.

"Apparently they are the people who planted us on Earth." Jason replied.

"And he used that phrase – planted?"

"Yes, sir. He did." Jason marveled for a moment that he remembered that part of the conversation.

"He also said there was a colony on Mars ages before the Denebians landed on Earth. That the Denebians were determined to wipe the Martians out and actually planted the seeds of their destruction."

"Now this is interesting. Did they give you an idea of how long ago this was?"

"Not really. I took it to be in the neighborhood of ten thousand years, at least." Jason rubbed his forehead, as if doing so would release more memories. "Apparently, the Denebians haven't tried to contact the Earth since that time. Tony seemed kind of concerned that they might come back and use the same techniques of annihilation if they find the Earth contaminated by the Martians. Does that make sense?"

O'Keefe nodded. "Seems their timing might be critical. Your alert message was just what we needed. They could have slipped past us if the Pegasus hadn't been sent to intercept. And we didn't want to send them if it appeared everything was ok. You understand how important your action was to us?"

"Yes, sir, I do. I was afraid at the time that Marsella was going to come in and interrupt me, but she didn't. I think it took them some time to get used to our bodies. She seemed to have a lot of trouble with it." He chuckled, remembering how she had gotten the two halves turned around when Tony slapped her around that one time.

"You think their kind will have problems assimilating Earth's population then?" O'Keefe asked.

"It depends on how much experience they can pass between them." Jason sat back and pondered for a minute.

O'Keefe finally broke in on his thoughts. "What are you thinking about, son?"

"Well, its just odd that they seemed to know so much about what we were doing," Jason sat bolt upright and shouted, "They can read thoughts!"

"Are you certain?" O'Keefe looked up as his staff filed into his office.

"I am positive." Jason affirmed. "They influenced our thoughts while we were on the planet. I distinctly remember Tony feeling as if there was something wrong and I thought so too, but then didn't think so. I'm sure they were manipulating us."

O'Keefe looked around the room at his staff. He didn't have to ask if they had gotten all that Jason had said. They had been monitoring the conversation from their individual stations. Captain Baldwin nodded her head. She concurred that Jason was at least mentally up for continued questioning.

The Colonel turned back to Jason on the monitor. "Jason, my staff has just assembled to deliberate some of the things you've told me. Are you certain their conversations are mostly mental?"

"Yes, sir. Tony, or whoever took over his body, often seemed distracted by something I couldn't hear. He answered Marsella a couple times without me hearing her question. I'm certain of that. They must be studied. They have capabilities we weren't even remotely prepared for."

"Acknowledged, Commander. What else can you tell us

about the Denebians?"

"Not much. Tony was concerned that they hadn't returned to check up on their charges for an extended amount of time. He never did say how long that time actually was."

"Did he give you any indication about their composition? Can we count on them being like us?"

"I don't know. I gathered that we were part of an experiment to see how we could adapt to different environments. The Martians at the time of our planting were upset that the Denebians would take over a planet that the Martians wanted to settle for themselves. I think they were miffed that the Denebians got their mitts in first."

"No indication why the Mars group didn't get here first? After all, they were in the same solar system."

Jason shook his head. "No, he was very close mouthed about some things. That may have been one topic he didn't want to discuss."

Captain Baldwin spoke for the first time. "Jason, how do you feel?"

"I feel fine, sir. In fact, I'm surprised I feel as good as I do, especially after the way they treated me."

"Acknowledged. We are frankly amazed as well. What do you attribute it to?"

"I don't right know. It isn't something I've had a chance to think about yet." Jason could barely see her in the monitor. What was she getting at? A cold knot settled into the pit of his stomach. He looked back at the Colonel.

"I'm not getting out of here any time soon, am I?"

O'Keefe shook his bushy head. "No, you aren't. I'm sorry, son. I know how much you want to get back to Molly and the kids but we can't let you go yet."

Captain Baldwin stepped in. "We think it possible you might have been changed by your ordeal."

"In what way?" Jason found himself demanding.

"Think it through for yourself," she said, then continued, "you are up walking around and feeling little affect from being savagely beat up. Not to mention how much blood your body lost to your vampires."

She said the last word with more than a little personal trepidation. All of her experience pointed to vampires as being fictional characters better left outside normal channels.

"Well, for the record, they aren't my vampires. And I frankly don't like where this conversation is headed. Did you find any contaminates in my body?"

"No, we didn't," she had to admit being puzzled, "you seem as healthy and red blooded as the rest of us." She looked at the Colonel. "I think that is what is really bothering me. He should still be suffering from the beating they put him through. But he is healthy and his visible wounds are even starting to disappear. I suggest we take this thing slowly."

"Has there been any change at the DNA level?" O'Keefe asked.

Captain Baldwin had to shake her head. "We found no indication of tampering."

"So Commander Martin could be released to limited duty?"

"I wouldn't make that recommendation, no. I think we need to wait out another quarantine cycle."

Jason felt his blood pressure rising. "You aren't the one locked up in this room, Captain. I am and I don't want to stay here any longer than is necessary." Jason turned back to the

Colonel. "Sir, I am ready to get out of here."

O'Keefe held up his hand to both sides of the monitor. He looked around the table where six other people sat. His glance passed over each of them in turn. Heads nodded or shook. Four shakes. Even if he wanted to rule in favor of Commander Martin, he couldn't justify it. There was too much at stake.

"I'll be getting back in contact with you tomorrow on that subject, Commander. Bear with us for a while longer. Ok?"

Jason sighed and leaned back. "Yes, sir. There seems to be nothing else I can do." He settled back and stared at a monitor now gone blank. They were stonewalling him. Some aspects of his health disturbed them.

Especially Captain Baldwin. She was spooked or he didn't know how to read people. 'That's really funny,' he thought. 'That never has been my strong point.' He got up and walked back over to his bed. Thoughts were flying through his head.

Captain Baldwin looked up from her brainwave computer screen and nodded to the Colonel. "He is not the same Commander we sent out there. His brain activity has peaked so far above Commander Martin's that I think we can prove just by that that we have one of them in our sickbay."

"You have to be certain." O'Keefe cautioned.

"I am certain."

"But you have scans and dissections from the others. Why is he so different from them? And can he infect anyone else with whatever he has?"

"We don't have answers to those questions yet."

Too many questions and not enough answers. O'Keefe suddenly felt his age. Somehow he was beginning to look forward to retirement. Three years couldn't pass too soon at this point. "I need answers, people."

17 ESCAPE

Captain Baldwin felt a tingling feeling in the back of her brain. She frowned and tried to concentrate on Commander Martin's charts. They were off the scale. There was no way he should have brain activity in areas typically dormant in the human race.

"Maybe they've figured some way to juice up their brains," she said to no one in particular. Everyone else had gone for the day. She distracted twirled her hair around the fingers of her right hand and again had to refocus her eyes.

'I shouldn't be having this much trouble with my eyes,' she complained to herself. The overheads were off and a strong spotlight on her desk provided light to the surface of her desk. Right where she liked it. She looked up and scanned the rest of her office in sickbay. Something was starting to get her nerves on edge.

"I should be wrapping up the day anyway." She looked at the chronometer her son had given her as a parting gift when she lifted off for her assignment to the Moon. His smiling picture was imbedded in the plastic on the left side. She looked behind him at the Maine coast scenery. Wind blown trees on the coast. Michelle suddenly realized how homesick she was. She wasn't up for rotation for another six months. 'Can't come too soon.'

"My feelings exactly," stated a male voice from the shadows in front of her desk. A shrill scream passed her lips as she pushed backwards out of her chair. "Who are you? Step forward and identify yourself. You almost scared me to death!"

"I apologize for that, Captain," Jason stepped forward and leaned over the front of her desk.

"You can't be here," she stated flatly, however, the quiver of fear was starting to come back into her voice. "You are supposed to be locked up in the quarantine ward. How? How did you get out?" She began reaching for the communications console on the side of her desk.

"Please don't do that." Jason's unusually smooth voice almost made her drop the receiver.

She replaced it into its spot and asked, "Why not?"

"Well, partially because I've disconnected it." Jason stepped back so his face became congealed in shadows once more. "It would be an operation in futility and I know how much you hate futile gestures. Just relax, Captain."

"What do you want?" she demanded.

"The same thing that you just desired so poignantly. I want to go home to my family. And you are going to arrange that." Jason pulled up the chair across from her desk and leaned on the back of it.

Michelle looked at him in silence for some time. Finally she lowered her head, no longer able to handle the frankness of his eyes. She knew this was not the reserved man who had commanded Mars Mission III. He had evolved.

"Yes, I have," his statement made her start. "I realized during that last briefing that there was something I hadn't considered. So I started doing some real thinking. Its surprising what the brain can come up with when it operates at full capacity. You were right about me, doctor. I have evolved. Just like the rest of the human race must if we are to survive."

"How's that?" she had been half-listening. The other half of her brain was occupied with getting notice to someone of her abduction.

"Captain, let me settle your mind for you. You have no chance in hell of contacting any of the chain of command. I'm going to walk out of here and you are going with me. No one is going to stop us. Got that?"

"If you're so certain, why do you need me?" she demanded.

"Because you already know too much for your own good," he stated matter of factly. "You are already in danger. I'm surprised O'Keefe has placed you under surveillance already. You are probably the one person on staff I would have monitored."

"Whatever are you talking about, Commander? I don't need to be watched. And speaking of watching. We placed cameras all over quarantine. How did you get past them?"

"Physical devices are easy to fool. Almost as easy as humans. You know we believe everything our eyes show us? We have been long overdue for some major improvements in that area."

The doctor stiffened her back. "I'm not taking you out of here." She looked him straight in the eyes and saw the truth even as she spoke.

"Yes. I think after you hear what I have to say you will." Jason sat back and steepled his hands in front of him. "Have you even stopped to consider the other half of the package that was brought back?" He waited.

"You mean the other creatures who came back with you?"

"Exactly." Jason moved forward and his face came into the circle of light. "If we, you and I, don't do something – they will.

And I don't think you want the result of their brand of ruling. Things would change drastically. And I mean drastic in earthquake terms of nine on the Richter Scale. The human race as we know it will be gone within twenty years, maybe less."

Michelle shivered. The prospect of allowing four creatures loose on an unsuspecting Earth was unnerving. She had had nightmares of such beasts after her brother took her to a Saturday afternoon matinee. To think they could be real was almost too much.

"That little niggling feeling you had at the base of your brain was Angela. She was trying to judge whether she could directly control you."

Startled, Michelle's head jerked up. Her eyes were wide as she stared back at him. "How did you know about that?" she demanded.

"I was deliberating about doing the same. Then I realized that I needed to take a more hands on approach. Fortunately for us that is something they can't yet do. I have to hand it to O'Keefe. He certainly thought of most things when he designed Moon Base X. It will take some time before they can get enough control subjects here to release them. That is why we have to hurry."

"What do you propose doing to stop them?"

"Oh, we aren't going to be able to stop them," Jason grinned as the startled look passed over her features again. "We have to evacuate every person from the Moon and do it soon."

"Do you know the monstrous task that would be?" she laughed harshly. "We couldn't evacuate even this station. Not even if we wanted to. There are over three thousand people on this one base. I'd estimate another sixteen thousand or so scattered around in the various facilities. You don't think getting you to Mars was a small undertaking, do you?"

"No I don't. But we have to try or you are going to have a lot of dead people up here and many more when Tony and his crew reach the Earth. The only way of keeping them from doing that is to deny them resources both here and there. Do you understand that?"

"Yes, Commander, I think I've got the gist of what you've been saying," she shook her head, suddenly feeling the full impact of her forty years. "There has to be some way of containing them."

"There isn't." The matter of fact way he delivered those two words scared her.

"Our technology is no match for their control of the mind and reality. Listen to me, Captain, we don't have anything that can approach them when it comes to understanding how to manipulate their environment. They have become masters – with a capital M on that word. Believe me."

"I do." Michelle Baldwin was stunned by how sure staff had been during their planning sessions. They couldn't have known the danger, but they had let a nest of vipers into the house. She was staring right at one.

The fact that he had escaped from quarantine was enough for her. She had personally designed most of the containment system in there herself. But he had walked right out of them, without setting off any alarms.

"And Angela can already get past most of the systems in place at Base X. She just hasn't figured out how to get around the flooding issue. She hates water so I don't know what she will do when she gets to Earth. Now that will be irony!"

Michelle looked up as Commander Martin started to excitedly pace back and forth. "Please, Commander, I don't think is the time to find something funny related to our situation."

Jason looked at her and calmed himself. "Of course. You are correct. But it would be ironic if they found they can't survive, but they are so adaptable."

"If you say so," Michelle looked up as Jason paused in front of her desk. "You are our expert here, Commander. Even though I'm not sure we should even allow you anywhere near an airlock."

"Granted, Captain. And under normal circumstances I would have to agree with you. I mean, I have been infected, haven't I. I know there are many reasons why I shouldn't go near Earth, but there are several reasons why I must. My family among them."

"Have you thought of them?" Michelle interjected. "How are they going to fare when you waltz back into their lives with a major virus running through your system?"

"I've actually thought about that," he replied, "I believe I will be doing Earth a favor by giving them a mild infection. Kind of like inoculating them." He looked hopefully at Michelle.

She nodded. "It might work. But you would have to come in contact with an awfully lot of people for your plan to be effective and you know how territorial most of those bozos down there are. It would take years to educate them."

"We don't have years, Captain. And I'm not going to be someone's lab rat for the rest of my life."

Michelle nodded again. "I'm starting to understand how you feel. So what is this plan of yours, Commander?"

Commander Martin was deep in thought. She had brought up a point he hadn't figured into his calculations. He had thought there would be many trips to make with standard shuttles and all, but close to twenty-four thousand people? That was too much. He hadn't realized how fast the Moon venture had grown.

"Can we isolate all the people who had anything to do with the design of Base X?" he asked her.

She shook her head. "Even if we could, there are still so many people scattered in temp shelters between here and there. It will take weeks to get everyone back inside Moon Base Alpha. And even then, where would we put them all? We couldn't support them."

Commander Martin agreed with her analysis of the situation. They were stuck if they couldn't come up with something better.

"We could take Tony and his crew aboard the Pegasus, disable its reactor and shove it toward the Sun. But I'm not even sure something that drastic would work."

"What do you mean?" she asked.

"I'm not certain they can even be killed by extreme heat. We might wake up some morning to find the same creatures amongst us but bearing distinct radioactive signatures."

"Well, then. What do we do?" Captain Baldwin looked hopefully at Jason.

He shrugged. "I don't know. An hour ago I had it all figured out. Now I'm not sure of anything. See what you've done to me, Michelle?"

"Don't blame me for that, mister." She pointed her finger at him and they both laughed. They finally subsided and looked at each other.

"There might not be a way out of this one," he concluded. "I'm not sure that is what you wanted to hear, but we might have just stepped on the big one this time."

Michelle was chilled by the prospect that he might be right. What if the human race had finally met something they couldn't control. They had always known the possibility existed that somewhere in space they would meet a race so totally opposed to humanity that the end was ensured. 'Could this be the one?' she thought.

18 PEGASIS IN FLIGHT

The outer airlock on the Pegasus hissed as air equalized. Commander Martin stood aside and let Captain Baldwin precede him into the tight chamber. Moments later green showed on the panel and the inner lock allowed them onto the flight deck. Jason was relieved to see that all systems had been left in station keeping mode. They would have to spend little time in working up for departure.

"You are sure you can drive this bus?" Michelle asked as she slipped into the co-pilot's seat and started her share of the pre-flight checks. Her attitude had changed since Jason had suddenly turned up in her office.

She knew from her own increased brain activity that she had become infected by just the short amount of time they had been in contact. She didn't yet know how, but it was possible that Jason's plan to infect the Earth might work. She shook her head as she checked switches and gauges.

'We are going to need luck to be on our side,' she thought. She looked over at Jason. He seemed to be so confident now. Not at all like the psych profile she had done on him prior to Mars III's departure.

"Yeah, I can drive the bus," he thought directly into her brain.

"See how easy it is to communicate when you don't have to worry about verbal getting in the way?"

"Yes, I do see," she marveled that she had never thought of telepathy as being possible before. "Are we always going to be like this?"

"It gets better with time," he said as he closed the switch that opened the dome in which the Pegasus was stored. They had about fifteen minutes before it would be opened enough for them to depart. To anyone watching they spent the time quietly. Inside their heads much was being communicated.

In his office Colonel O'Keefe sat back and placed his fingers on the tender spot beneath his right ear. Touching the stud just under the skin produced a tone that alerted the visitors that all was proceeding as planned. He received a lower tone back which he had come to recognize as their acknowledgement.

"I hope this is the right thing to do," he said to no one but himself. He had gotten into the habit of talking to himself since coming to the Moon posting. He sighed and looked at the pictures of Earth on his desk. It would change drastically if he were wrong. But he agreed with everything that Commander Martin had vocalized. They needed to beat the other guys to the punch. That seemed to be what the visitors were after also.

O'Keefe watched the monitor as the Pegasus lifted off. Commander Martin would be given a head start before base personnel were alerted to their departure. Then things would get busy as people rushed here and there trying to come up with some method of intercepting the craft before it could enter Earth's atmosphere.

O'Keefe would have to play his part. He sighed again, got to his feet and went into the briefing room. There he waited.

On the dark side of the Moon things were different. Angela had learned late in the game that Commander Martin was out of quarantine. He was already inserting the Pegasus in near Earth transit before she picked up his brain activity. 'Its almost like he hid himself from us,' she told the others.

Tony was furious. He was still angry over the way they had been treated by the humans. 'We would have treated them better if they had visited our planet,' he remarked.

'They did. And look how we treated them,' Marsella pointedly said. She walked over to where he was sitting and posed before him. 'We invited ourselves to dinner.'

She expected Tony to rise to the bait. He didn't. Instead, he and Angela were deep in a conversation about how to escape from their prison. Marsella huffed for a moment, then walked off. But her posture showed she didn't like being ignored.

Jason looked up from the astrogation console as his comms board came to life. 'Right on time,' he stated to Michelle. "Roger, Moon Base Alpha. We've been expecting your call. This is Commander Martin. What can I do for you?"

"Commander, this is Kim Wang. I have Colonel O'Keefe standing by," she looked back over her shoulder as the Colonel leaned toward the video camera.

"Commander, you have seriously endangered Earth and all of us with your actions. This is a direct order. You are to turn the Pegasus around, land at Moon Base Alpha, and shut down all systems. Do you understand those orders, Commander?"

"Yes, sir. I understand them, but I can't comply. I can't explain right now, but it is imperative that I make it to Earth before Tony and his crew do."

"You realize this course of action can get you shot on sight?"

"Yes, sir. I understand the implications of my actions."

"And does Captain Baldwin also concur with what you are doing?"

"Yes, Colonel, I do. Jason has to be given safe passage to Earth. If we can…"

"Stow it, Captain," O'Keefe interrupted brusquely. "The only thing I want from you two is for you to power down and wait to be picked up. There is no room for discussion in this. Have I made myself clear?"

Jason reached for the switch to terminate communications, but hesitated. There was something lacking in the Colonel's approach. He couldn't quite put his finger on it. Michelle toned in. 'I felt it also. He should have been hopping mad that we stole one of his spacecraft. He wasn't.'

'You're right. Play back everything he said to us. He said there is no room for discussion in this. I've never heard him say anything like that before. Either he is slipping or trying to give us a head start.' They both looked at each other, then turned to the navigation boards again.

'How much can we get out of this bucket?' Jason asked absently. 'I'm betting that the Colonel is going to hold up pursuit for another half hour or so. They have at least two more of these cruisers sitting on the tarmac back there. Are they ready for the run? That's the question.'

'Can you scan them to see if anyone is onboard?' Michelle ventured.

Jason was silent, staring into near space for a few moments. 'They are fully loaded and ready to come up to power on command. Appears they're just waiting for the order. So what is O'Keefe playing?'

He faced Michelle, who shrugged. 'I haven't a clue. This thing could be bigger than we thought.'

Jason sat back and put his brain in gear. A cold knot grew with each passing moment. The thought that he almost broadcast to Captain Baldwin stopped in its tracks. He didn't even want to sub-vocalize it. The unthinkable ramifications of it were staggering and his face must have shown it.

"Jason, what is it?" demanded Michelle aloud. "You look like someone just walked over your grave."

'I think they did,' was all he would venture. He passed a cryptic look at her and she changed to non-verbal speech again.

'Don't say anything aloud unless I ask for it specifically. All of our urgent comms have to be done this way, but we have to keep up chatter for whatever listening devices have been placed onboard. They probably put visual devices too. I would if I were going to let my cruiser get hijacked.'

'But I don't see it. Shouldn't we be able to find it?'

'Not necessarily. I've been thinking about that. I've been out of touch with Earth for two years now. I might not even recognize it if I saw it.'

'But there should be an open frequency for transmitting the data back, don't you think?' Michelle was looking around the cockpit but came up empty. Jason also came up empty with his scan for the frequency.

'If they have a dedicated frequency it isn't active. We'll just have to wait on it,' he returned his attention to ensuring the correct burn vectors were fed into the navigation computers.

His attention was broken by a blip back on the Moon's surface. 'They've lifted off,' he told Michelle. Vocally he complained, "I wonder what they're waiting on. Colonel O'Keefe should have contacted us by now."

His mind was focused on what was occurring back at Moon Base Alpha. Two pursuit cruisers had lifted off the surface. They were still waiting for orders. Jason scanned them. What he found surprised him. They looked like the Pegasus on the outside but inside was another story.

They were armed with some very lethal looking burst type weapons. He didn't want to think about what those would do to any unarmored ship or its occupants. They also had oversized drives. They could catch the Pegasus after even an eight hour head start. He was certain of that. 'What are we playing with here?' he asked himself again. 'We have to get answers.'

19 DECISION TIME

'Turning around is not an option,' Jason thoughtfully considered all of his options. They were perhaps midpoint between the Moon and Earth. Three hours earlier he had reduced their speed to a crawl. Their pursuers also had done the same.

'O'Keefe is giving me room to maneuver. The question is why? What is he hoping that I'll discover on my own?' That question had been bugging him for some time. Ever since he and Michelle Baldwin escaped Moon gravity, he had been thinking about it.

'They allowed us to escape and you know it,' Michelle finished his thought for him. They looked at each other then out the window in front of them at the Earth view that was holding steady. The blue-green and browns beckoned to them both. 'We can't do this,' she continued, 'We aren't some monsters who can infect that beautiful planet down there,' her voice trailed off in his head. He allowed her to have the privacy of her mind. But he now realized that he agreed.

They sat in silence for some time. "Michelle, I'm sorry I got you into this," he said aloud finally. "I had no right to infect you." She glanced over at him and saw the big tears flowing from his eyes. Reaching over she patted his hand. "It's OK," was all she could manage.

Both were suddenly shocked out of their wits by the intrusion.

Tony's mind was present in the cockpit with them. 'You two lovebirds are really breaking my heart. Meanwhile, those who could be your mentors are stuck back here in the darkness. Snap out of it, fools! There's work to be done and you sit there sniveling about your precious Earth. I never will fully understand your ability to self-destruct.'

Jason's back stiffened. 'How are you doing this? They placed a dampening field around Moon Base X. You shouldn't be able...'

Tony rudely interrupted. 'We have some of the best minds NASA could buy right here in the midst of us, dear boy. Remember that Buzz and Amanda were both trained by the same people who constructed this forsaken site. They were able to reverse the polarity on the field so we can now communicate to the very edge of the solar system if we needed to. Feels like I'm right there with you, doesn't it?'

'What do you want?' Jason drove right to the point. His mind was beginning to feel accosted by the other man. 'I feel like I need to take a shower every time he thinks at me,' he tight beamed to Michelle. 'I know what you mean,' she shot back, 'but keep him talking. We might find out what they're up to.'

Jason nodded and opened his mind again. Tony was already detailing part of his plan. 'need to turn around and pick us up,' he was saying. Jason crowded in on him. 'Any outside action taken to release you will result in the explosion of at least ten nuclear devices. That place is wired to blow if there is any tampering with the containment system. The military boys did their job. You aren't going anywhere.'

'That shows how short sighted your people are. Listen, Jason. We can already contain the explosions. Thanks for letting us know how many we need to worry with. You see, we weren't made privy to the plans like you were. Just hold on a minute while I check with my crew...' The link went dead but not before Jason felt the hesitation that Tony wasn't about to allow him to feel.

He tight beamed Michelle. 'Tony was scared. They can't contain that many devices and he knows it. He only has four people. I think I know how he will try it, but there are too many of them. Besides, it will only take one device to vaporize the base. Plus, I don't think he knows about the cruisers we saw. He isn't going anywhere.'

'I hope you're right,' she beamed back.

They waited until Tony finally came back into focus. 'Listen, gang. We have all the angles covered now. It's time for you two to turn that crate around and pick us up. We are ready to go home.'

The simplicity of the statement stunned Jason. 'That's it! That is exactly where we need to go!'

Michelle looked at him with growing consternation written all over her face. She could barely contain the tight beam on her thought patterns. 'We can't go there,' she started to protest, but Tony interrupted them.

'Are you two able to hide your thoughts from me?' he asked, then continued, 'We don't need any secrets in the coven and you two both know it.' His tone was chiding but bordered on becoming obsessed. 'Now get your asses moving!'

Jason folded his arms across his chest. 'No,' was all he had to say to provoke Tony into rage. They waited as the creature fumed and rampaged within the confined space they were in at Moon Base X. Finally there was quietness.

'They can't physically make us do anything,' he beamed to Michelle. 'We are on almost the same level with them ability wise, so they can't make us obey them. I'm just afraid that they can find some weak minds at one of the outlying bases who will help them.'

'Now that's a scary thought,' Michelle thought back. She glanced over at Jason. 'Were you really serious when you said we needed to go back to Mars?'

'As a matter of fact, I was,' he answered, 'I just wish I knew what is going through the General's mind right now. What does he have planned?' It was his turn to consider his companion. A new thought had occurred to him. 'Michelle, you were a member of the General's staff. What is he doing? More to the point, what does he want us to do?'

She sat looking out the window at the Earth view as if she hadn't heard his questions. Finally she sighed, 'I think he wants us to do exactly what we are doing,' she stated flatly. 'Somehow, I think we are supposed to lure those creatures back to their own planet. But how?'

'I don't know,' Jason had to admit. 'If we go back for them it becomes four against two and I've dealt with those odds before. That isn't an option. And keeping them locked up isn't very viable either. At some point they're going to escape and Earth will suffer. Those creatures are a plague that we have to contain – at all costs.'

His grim determination wasn't lost on her. Michelle countered, 'Why can't we just allow them to blow themselves up?' she started, but stopped as Jason shook his head.

'We can't allow that. They would simply become radioactive spoors that we wouldn't be able to clean up or contain. That also is not an option. I think that is Tony's backup plan. He will accept that because he knows that at least a percentage of the spoors will make it through our atmosphere. There's also something else at work here.'

She looked expectantly across the short distance separating them. Her eyebrows went up as he continued, 'I don't think Tony wants us to survive without him. He is wanting us to turn around so we are caught in whatever blast gets him. He knows he can't contain that many devices.'

'So he is going to get us with them,' she added. 'Why?'

'My question exactly. And I think the answer lies back on the Martian surface. Are you game for a jaunt into the hinterland, my dear?'

Michelle laughed for the first time in days. 'Yes, but I didn't pack anything to wear. Do you think they will be expecting us?'

'I don't know the answer to that one. Let's get this expedition on the road.'

20 DISCOVERY

"Your Worship. Begging your pardon. We know where Bartam and Barsomme are located now." Amadeus bowed his head and waited for his King to acknowledge his statement. Shadows lengthened before King Leopold the Third looked his way.

"Amadeus," he sighed. "Why do I put up with you? Can you tell me that? Your staff was supposed to have contained those two. Explain to me what happened."

The King's advisor swallowed a knot that threatened to choke his vocal cords. He didn't know quite how to answer. It had become apparent during his investigation that his crew of infiltrators had underestimated their quarry. Bartam had convinced them all that he was no longer a threat to the court. His early departure into stasis had taken him off the list of those who were monitored.

"Amadeus, I'm waiting."

"I'm truly sorry, your Worship. We took Bartam off the monitoring list when he went into stasis. We didn't consider him a threat," he stammered and felt a full, green blush coming on.

"Sire, we thought we had him contained."

"But, it's obvious you didn't." Leopold sat back and let his long arms drape over the sides of his throne. He really didn't want the head of his security chief, but protocol almost demanded it. The security of the throne was at stake here, he reasoned, but even that didn't sound convincing.

After all, he and Amadeus had been grown from chrysalis together. It was only by quirk of added genes that he was King and Amadeus was standing with his head bowed. But discipline had been slipping of late. Someone would have to pay. It was always up to him to figure out that angle. His crown suddenly chafed as it sat upon his royal brow.

He sighed again. "Amadeus, we have to make an example out of someone here. And you are the one ultimately in charge of the security of my throne. Who do you think we should punish for this 'oversight'?" His green eyes narrowed as Amadeus squirmed under the steady gaze of his King.

Amadeus slowly raised his head and considered his liege. Under other circumstances he probably would have been put to death immediately just for casting his eyes on the same level with the King. This was extraordinary and he had to make the King understand that.

His gaze didn't waver. "I take full responsibility for the entire affair," he said, then hurriedly continued, "but we aren't going to have a lot of time to train a new person to take my place. You need to be made aware of the extent of the damage in this case. I beg you to listen and then if you want my head you can have it once we meet the danger that has come upon us from those two." He swallowed hard, shocked at his own words.

His King sat up straight and leaned toward him. No friendliness was now evident in his demeanor or voice. "I will make that determination, Amadeus. I'm aware of how long you've been in my service and how long it would take to train someone else. But don't let that make you think you are not expendable."

"Yes, my Lord." Amadeus bowed his head once more and looked at his feet. The shock of speaking his mind was beginning to sink in. Had he really been that bold? In all his years of service he had never even heard of anyone being that direct with the King. It just didn't happen.

Leopold looked at the retainers standing against the wall and realized why Amadeus was still holding his tongue. He nodded at them and one lowered a switch recessed in the wall beside his station.

A shimmering shield fell around the area of the throne. Both felt the static that always accompanied the use of the shield. Nothing could be heard by those outside of the shield's perimeter. They could still see their King, and could react to any untoward action by anyone inside the circle of silence, but could hear nothing.

The King nodded for Amadeus to continue. "Now tell me about our two friends. Where are they?"

This was the moment of truth. Amadeus steeled himself. "They are off-planet, your Worship. They hijacked that last probe sent to us by the Third-Worlders."

"Damnation! Are you sure?" Amadeus could see consternation on the King's face. It was totally unthinkable that anyone would perpetrate such a crime. Mars's society had been brought along on the idea that those from the Third World could discover no trace of Martian society. It was ingrained into their children. The fact that Bartam would even consider it was obscene.

"Yes, there is no doubt that they overcame the crew and were transported at least as far as the moon of the Third Planet. We have intercepted communications between Bartam and at least one member of the probe's crew. Bartam was attempting to coerce the other one into assisting him in his plans to reach the Third World. They call it 'Earth', by the way."

"Amadeus, I really don't care what they call it. I want to know two things. How much has been compromised and are the Denebians involved?"

"I believe most of Earth's upper echelon know of our presence now. As for the Denebians, I can't say. They haven't made their presence known to the Earth people." He hedged by saying, "Not that we have seen, that is."

Leopold was silent for several minutes. "And Bartam? What is he doing? What are his plans, do you think?"

Amadeus had to shake his head. "We don't know. But I think we are going to find out soon. Another probe is on its way here and it has the other creature that I mentioned."

His King took note of Amadeus' turn of a phrase. "Why do you call it a creature, my friend?"

"Because it doesn't pass the spectro-analysis as being someone from the Third World. I think Bartam might have done something to this creature and has made him like one of us."

"You know that is impossible," Leopold waved his hand at the very thought. "Can they evolve into something higher than what we've seen? They've always appeared to be pretty fragile to me. Mostly water based, wouldn't you think?"

"Yes, sire. But we know that Bartam assimilated the body of one of the crew members and has inhabited it since they took over the ship."

The King's eyes narrowed. "Why wasn't I informed of this immediately?"

"You have been, your Majesty. I just found out before coming in for this audience."

"This changes everything. You know that? How soon until the probe arrives?"

"About two of our cycles. And yes, I realize that."

"Well, let's hope this can be contained." Amadeus looked at his King and realized something else. The guardians weren't going to be pleased by what the King would relate in his midnight cleansing ritual. He was suddenly glad he wasn't the King.

21 THE DEAL

'Now here's the deal,' Bartam, who inhabited the body of Tony, was directing his thoughts for the benefit of those on the Pegasus. 'You will turn around and pick us up. Otherwise things are going to get nasty.' He paused to give Jason a chance to think about the implications.

Jason looked at Captain Baldwin. She shrugged. She considered Bartam's posturing and blustering as just that. He couldn't escape and there really wasn't anything he could do that would change that. Jason was about to say as much when Bartam refreshed his memory.

'Remember those nuclear devices your people stashed up here? Let Amanda fill you in on the impact they will make.'

Amanda entered the communications path and hurriedly got to the point. 'Commander, here's the deal. There are twelve devices. Enough explosive power by themselves to cause some grave damage to the rest of the Moon installations your people have up here. I've added some refinements to the mix,' she paused for a moment, 'that mixture will create a combined explosion that will split your moon in half. Consider for a moment the chaos that is going to cause on Earth. The wobble alone will cause tidal waves like your planet has never experienced.'

Jason looked as if he had been kicked in the gut. 'You can't seriously think this is your best idea. Too many people will die, needlessly.'

'Then turn around,' Bartam stated flatly. 'We want to return to our own planet and you were just headed that way. The deal is, you take us back and drop us off. We will allow you to return to your precious Earth. No one will be hurt. But be aware that we will do just as Amanda detailed. Your moon will tear your planet apart and you will be the ones responsible. You have one hour.'

The connection was broken abruptly.

Michelle whispered to Jason, "You aren't going to do as he asked, are you?"

"We don't seem to have any choice. Amanda is capable of doing just as she said. She doesn't bluff. That is one of the reasons I selected her for the mission. No, she can do it and there is nothing we can do to contain it. We have to contact O'Keefe immediately." He reached for the comms channel switch and flipped it to active.

"This is Pegasus calling Moon Base Alpha. Commander Jason Martin speaking. Please open a secure channel to General O'Keefe."

"This is Captain Wang, Commander. The General will be right with you. Give me a moment."

"Roger, Captain." Jason sat back and looked at Earth, then reached across the space between the command chairs. "Can you get the astrogation computer set up or do you need some help with it?"

"I might need a little refresher when we get into the trajectories. Just a bit rusty but it should come back to me pretty quick." She set about powering up the astrogation equipment and watched closely as sub-screens began to appear on her main monitor. "Jason, will they really do it?" she asked in a timid voice.

Jason nodded. "Yes, I think they will. Bartam's back is against the proverbial wall and nothing will be gained by trying to stonewall him. He is holding a trump card here."

Jason jumped as the comms channel crackled. "This is General O'Keefe. Commander Martin, are you ready to turn about?"

"Yes, sir. We are ready to come about. Can you clear a path back to Moon Base X for us?"

"You aren't seriously thinking about going anywhere near there, are you?"

"We have to, General. Just listen to me for a moment." Jason suddenly didn't care if he had a secure channel or not. "We must return to base and pick up the creatures we've got penned there. We don't have a choice if you want to remain alive and if you don't want to see all life on Earth destroyed."

"Break it down slowly for me, Commander." General O'Keefe sat back and gazed across his desk at staff members who were just now getting to their positions. "We need to hear what you know."

Jason took a deep breath and smiled at Michelle for the first time in what seemed like ages. He decided to jump right in. "They have added something to the mix. The nuclear devices have been tampered with. Amanda assured me that they can now set an explosion that will split the Moon in half. You can imagine the destruction that will cause when the wobble starts upsetting Earth. You'll ride two gigantic rocks down to a couple enormous explosions, if you're unlucky enough to live that long."

"We get the picture, Commander. How long have they given you to respond?"

"An hour. We have about fifty minutes left before Tony calls me back."

"And you think he will do it? It would also mean his death. Do you really think he would do that?"

"Yes, sir. He will do it, but you are wrong about him dying. I'm not sure he can be killed. At least not in our sense of speaking. He and his people will simply encase themselves within a force field of some sort and drift as spoors from the middle of the explosion. They will land on Earth after the chaos has settled down and rule over what is left of our civilizations."

"Acknowledged, Commander. Give us a couple minutes to consider the implications of letting them walk out of there." The line went dead, but didn't stay that way long. It seemed to Jason that the General's staff didn't have to consider long.

"Very well, Commander. We are going to give you escort back to Moon Base X. Fall into formation with the Argus. They should be alongside shortly. Now let me talk with Captain Baldwin on secure."

Commander Martin indicated his acknowledgement of orders and got up to move into the back of the Pegasus. He didn't hear Captain Baldwin's conversation.

"Captain, can we set these creatures down on Earth and keep them quarantined?"

"Negative," the shock in her voice was apparent. "We can't even come anywhere near Earth. General, Commander Martin didn't tell you everything. You hardly gave him a chance to. We have changed."

"What do you mean, you've changed? What have you changed?"

She swallowed, then plunged in, "We have been changed into whatever those creatures are. We are like them now. I think the fact that the Commander is alive amazed them, but something changed his physiology and when he broke into my office I became infected with it. We can't go anywhere near Earth. Anyone coming into contact with us is going to become infected. And I don't know what the full impact would be."

"You're telling us you two are evolving? How can that happen?"

"I think this is what the creatures had in mind all along, General. They want to infect the Earth with a virus of some sort, but they want to do it with them in control. They want to feed on us like we are the sheep."

That sunk in. The General looked at his staff. Captain Robertson had been doing intense analysis on the Commander's blood work. He nodded. General O'Keefe continued, "Then we must assume there is only one recourse available to us here." He made his decision. "Captain, can you ensure the Pegasus can never lift off again once you reach Mars?"

"Yes, sir. I know some tricks that will ensure that. What is your plan?"

"We have to contain these creatures at all cost. The problem is that we don't know how many of them are living on the surface, or below the surface, of Mars. But we can't allow them to even think about coming back this way. If what you say is true, then you are going to live the rest of your natural life with them. We need to know what we are dealing with. And I can't ask you to volunteer. You are Earth's last hope."

Michelle looked out at the crescent shape of Earth on her left shoulder and realized how much she wanted to go home. "I understand, General."

Minutes later Jason slid back into the command chair. "What did the General want with you?" he asked.

Michelle wiped her eyes and looked at him. *'Don't make me tell you lies,'* she thought at him. "He wanted to get my take on what you've become," she said aloud.

"Then let's get this done and deliver some cargo back to Mars, shall we?" He steeled himself for the task at hand.

22 RETURN TO MARS

Amanda sat up. 'Our ride is here,' she shouted without making a sound. Everyone mobilized. They had already planned down to the last detail. Amanda looked from Buzz to Tony and smiled. They were moments away from freedom.

Jason's thoughts broke into theirs. 'Leave everything on the deck and enter the loading bay one at a time. Bring anything with you and I'll have you placed in deep freeze again and I know you don't want that.'

Bartam caustically cut him off. 'We know the drill, Commander. We are on our way out. Just keep your boys from becoming trigger-happy. And Commander, there will be some extra refinements that we will be bringing back with us. Call them souvenirs of your world.'

Jason looked at Captain Baldwin and tight beamed the thought, 'Can you get a scan of what he is talking about…' he didn't get the thought completed. She had turned white.

'Commander, they each have a device on their backs. There are no triggers or anything like that. It's all mind controlled. If they release the shield we will cause one big explosion in space.'

'Listen to her, Commander. We are going back to Mars on our terms. Your people can deep-freeze us all they want. The resultant explosion will

cook everything in the vicinity and I don't think you want that. Now get the hatch open so we can be off this cursed little ball of leftover space dust.'

Jason flipped the switch for the entry portal and watched his new companions disappear beneath the hull. He heard their footsteps on the deck behind him. Three sets.

He got up from the command chair as Tony entered the forward cabin. "Where is Marsella?" he demanded, starting to move past Tony.

Tony reached out and detained him against the bulkhead. "Don't worry yourself about her. Her worthless body will be staying behind." Yellow-green eyes stared deep into Jason's.

"Let's just say I owed her for making you what you are. We would be safely tucked away from prying eyes upon your precious Earth if she hadn't interfered. Now, let's get this bucket pointed outbound for Marsoome."

Jason sat back in the command chair and nodded to Michelle. She toggled the pre-flight switches and called toward the back of the craft. "Strap yourselves in. Flight in five minutes and counting."

Tony moved toward the back, taking Amanda with him. Buzz remained positioned with his legs spread under his shoulders, just behind the command module. His keen eyes didn't miss a thing that went on.

Michelle wished he would join the others, but knew that wasn't going to happen. She settled back in her seat and concentrated on getting them into space once again. Jason had taken over the astrogation duties and appeared not to notice anyone else.

Finally he sat back and punched in the engage key that passed the necessary information to Michelle's console computer. She felt the engines power up and pulled the yoke back to release the gravity well that had kept them pinned to the metal landing apron. They bobbed slightly for a moment, and then Jason applied thrust into the drive pod. They were on their way.

Buzz relaxed as they lifted into space and came around to join the Argus. 'Is that ship going to tail us all the way?' he asked.

Jason turned his head and said aloud, "I don't know what the General has in mind. They may go with us. I haven't been informed." He fell silent as three more Pegasus class cruisers joined the Argus. "I guess that kind of answers your question, huh?"

Buzz went into the rear compartment and joined his friends. Michelle looked at Jason. 'You are such a liar,' she chided in their tight-beamed connection. 'You know the General won't let them anywhere near Earth now.'

'Yes, I know that. But I'm hoping Tony doesn't and if we can keep him off balance for a while we might be better off.' He cut the connection as Tony and Amanda came forward.

Time for us to lay down some ground rules for you two lovebirds. We are the ones who make decisions from now on. No argument. We tell you to do something we want it done, without question. Got that?'

Jason shrugged. 'Maybe I do, maybe not. You have to realize that you don't hold all the cards you think you do. Those four cruisers out there are going to accompany us for a good reason. We are going one place and any departure from the flight path will result in all four of them opening fire. They will ensure atoms are the only things that will come from the ensuing firefight. Got that?'

Jason didn't realize that he had gotten up from his command chair. He and Tony were now standing nose to nose, neither willing to back down. Amanda finally decided to get between them. "Listen, you two turkeys can prance all you want. Commander, we just want to get back home without anyone killing anyone. I'm going to get some rest."

She walked toward the back, looking over her shoulder. "You coming?" she asked Tony. He nodded slightly, then turned back to Jason. "You screw with me and only one of us will make it home." Jason shrugged again and sat down, but looked back down the passageway.

His eyes said a mouthful as they met Michelle's. 'We have to watch it around those two. Don't know about Buzz and I wish I knew where Marsella was. I know he didn't kill her. So what is she up to?'

As if to answer his question, the world suddenly went black. Concussion from the fireball lifting from the moon's surface hit them a moment later. Jason finally was able to lift his head. He scanned his board.

The EMP had wiped out all his circuits. He reached under the console and toggled a switch that engaged the backup circuitry. Since they hadn't been activated during the blast, they weren't affected by the pulse. He scanned his navigation screen as circuits came on. All four of his escorts were still with them. They also had been hit by the pulse but were reporting in.

Tony came into the cockpit area and looked out at the fireball that was still lifting from the Moon. "That will keep them busy for a while, don't you think?"

Michelle half-rose from her seat, a feral look in her eyes. Jason shouted at her, "Belay that action, Captain! Sit down and concentrate on getting us back on line. That's an order!"

She sat back but both men noticed the intense hatred that had blossomed in her eyes. Tony knew he had made an enemy he didn't really need. Jason realized he would have to keep an eye on her as well as the others.

He looked at Tony. "Why?"

"We had to show the fatheads that we mean business. What better way than to make things hell for a while. They'll have quakes and repairs for days. Besides, we thought maybe we could take out a couple of those escorts out there. Hadn't figured on the backup systems. And bless Marsella's little heart, she was late in triggering the explosion. To the end, she couldn't get it right."

"You are a heartless bastard," Michelle almost came out of her chair again, but held up, as Jason's look warned her to sit back down.

"Well, my dear, you have to have a heart to be without one. I never had one to start with. You see, I'm what is known as a criminal on my own world. I've had centuries to plan this little foray. And now you've delivered into my hands exactly what I've needed to bring my plans to fruition. You're going to land me on my planet with enough fire power to declare myself in charge — and make it stick."

Jason and Michelle shuddered as they considered the devices the three Martians had attached to their backs. If the explosion that was still visible from their vantage point above the Moon's surface was any indication of what Tony had in mind, both wanted nothing to do with it.

"Well, let's not wait around all day. Get under way, Commander."

The Pegasus moved toward its destiny with Mars, followed closely behind by a fleet of cruisers whose crews were now steeled to do whatever they had to do to ensure no Martian would every step foot on Earth.

23 AMADEUS AND LEOPOLD

"Your Worship. They are on their way." Amadeus wasn't sure he had been heard, but the King turned his way. Yellow-green eyes stared balefully at him. The King was in one of his dark moods. The grimace that turned down his lips convinced Amadeus that he was in serious danger if he said or did the wrong thing at the wrong moment. Leopold was known as being hard to handle at the best of times. With recent events, his schizoid side had come out more and more. He was slowly going mad.

Amadeus stepped back into his alcove and lowered his eyes. His Majesty's words were slurred and almost too quiet.

"Amadeus, we have seriously misjudged this situation. I'm afraid we have reached a period when grave concern will become the lot of all the people. And it all started with your botched security efforts. I should just have your head. You know that?"

He stared for a long moment at his advisor's contrite form. But the madness of the moment had passed. Even he couldn't in cold blood take the life force of another being.

The King lifted his long arms over his head and scratched his topknot. His yellow and black fangs protruded from the sides of his broad mouth as he stretched his facial features by pulling upwards on the knot. That action always served to calm his emotions. He was smiling as he reseated himself on his throne and indicated that Amadeus was to approach.

"Inform your King of the events you alluded to. And, Amadeus. I want to hear it all. Nothing watered down. I need to make decisions and to make them, I need all the information you gathered."

"Yes, your Worship. You know of course about the explosion that took place on the Third World's moon. It appears that one of the beings that Bartam infected decided to stay behind and set off something they call a nuclear device."

Amadeus had approached as closely as he dared. Males of their species never came into close contact. Serious discords could erupt whenever they did, so circles were drawn into every floor letting each know they hadn't entered someone else's space.

"We intercepted a communication between the original probe and his superiors on their moon. It appears he was given permission to pick up Bartam and Barsomme. We have to assume they are in human form."

"Why do you say that?" Leopold leaned forward, interested in why his advisor would make that conclusion.

"Because we tapped into Bartam's conversation with the Earth creature where he was complaining about how frail his Earth body was. That he had to sleep more than what he thought was normal."

Leopold interrupted him. "What is this sleep?"

Amadeus gave his version of a shrug. "We figure it is something like our stasis. Where they lay down and actually become unconscious. Earth's people do it when the sun goes down on their half of the Third World. We don't know what it does for them. Personally I think it is a serious weakness for nature to require such cycles in the conscious state. We might be able to study it once we get the creatures here."

"That will have to be a side issue, Amadeus." Leopold rubbed his chin with his long fingers and stared into space. "What else did you learn?"

"That the two creatures who picked up Bartam were the ones who landed in the probe and that somehow Bartam is responsible for at least one of them becoming a hybrid creature."

Leopold's eyes sparkled. "I'm going to look forward to receiving Bartam's head once he arrives. He has some serious debts to pay." His teeth clashed together and he stood and strode toward Amadeus.

For his part, Amadeus shrieked and jumped back a circle to allow the King to occupy the one he had just been standing in. His heartbeat surged as he realized the danger he had been in. The King's claws could have disemboweled him easily. He shivered as the King returned to the area of his throne and indicated that he was once more to occupy the advisor's circle.

"You are correct to be cautious, Amadeus. Is there anything else we need to know before the creatures deliver Bartam back into our hands?"

"Yes, your Majesty, there is. The original probe has at least four other of their warships coming with it. They could mean trouble. I witnessed their firepower earlier as two of them went through their shakedown cruises within our space. You remember the video feed we made of that event?"

Leopold had to think back. It had been several cycles since he had seen them. Now he remembered the long and short-range bombardment the Earth vessels had made on a rogue asteroid. It had been vaporized. His scientists were convinced there was no shield within their arsenal that could withstand such firepower. So they had to be careful.

"Yes, I remember that sequence. And you think they are going to be looking for a fight once they arrive in orbit?"

"Why else would they send so many of them, your Worship?"

"Why indeed? What is it they really want to accomplish? Their probes, both manned and unmanned, have seemed to be peaceful enough. Wasn't that your assessment during their last mission here?"

"That was. Bartam seems to have hit a nerve with them. It seems they are intensely terrified that he might actually make it to their planet. The mission leader was detailing that to his superiors on his way back to their moon. It seems that Bartam would possess powers much enhanced once he reached Earth. He would become as a god amongst their people. Or that is what their leader was afraid of."

The King hung his head. "Why did this have to happen during my years? Amadeus, we have seriously underestimated this entire situation. I looked over your analysis of Bartam. He is borderline on all characteristics. His isn't a positive profile on any point. He isn't intelligent enough to pull something off of this magnitude. What did we miss?"

"I'm in agreement with you to a point, your Majesty. But consider this. He is now co-joined with someone from their world. And they only send their brightest into space. They are highly trained and would provide a springboard for even Bartam's limited intelligence."

"Enough!" Leopold's eyes flashed. "You are not making sense now, Amadeus. How can that be possible? Are you saying he assimilated their natural intelligence into his own?"

"I'm afraid so, sire. You asked for everything."

"Yes, I know I did," Leopold sat heavily onto his throne. "We are in serious trouble if even part of that is possible." He heaved a heavy shudder and stood up. "Amadeus, get those scanners on line and get me some concrete evidence that we don't have to worry about Bartam suddenly being intelligent."

"Yes, sire. I'll let you know as soon as we have something." He backed out of the throne room and ran toward the communications rooms. There wasn't a moment to be wasted.

Behind him, King Leopold sat back wearily on his throne. His advisor was correct in one thing. There wasn't much time to be wasted. He was suddenly tired and wished he could take his turn in stasis, but he knew it wouldn't happen for too many cycles. His duty to his people weighed heavily on his shoulders.

They had successfully dealt with those from the Third World in the past. As far as he knew, they weren't even aware that there flourished a civilization of high caliber upon Marsomme. Or they hadn't.

"Bartam has changed all of that," he stated to the air in front of him. "Well, we can't go back now. We'll have to see how this plays out."

24 DISCUSSION WITH HOME

Captain Baldwin flipped the comms channel switch off. "Are you sure you're up to this?" she asked. Jason's face was ashen and drawn. He looked like he hadn't slept for days.

He nodded resolutely and wiped his hand across his face. "I have to talk to her. You understand that, don't you?"

Michelle looked out at the ovoid that was the Argus on their port bow and smiled a sad smile. She turned back toward him. "She is, after all, your wife. The mother of your children. How could I not understand?"

Jason smiled for the first time in days. "Even knowing that we will probably be an item for the rest of our natural lives? I know I can never see her again, but you know that she will always be in my heart."

"I know that," she said quietly. "If it were any other way, I wouldn't feel the attraction I do toward you. I have to know that you are going to stand by your convictions. Even if I have to compete with her memory for the rest of my life."

She reached across the cabin and patted his arm as she got up. "Talk with her. She needs you to tell her." With that Michelle moved into the back cabin.

Jason sat there for several minutes before he could get up enough courage to flip the channel open. "Moon Base Alpha, this is Commander Martin. Is my wife standing by?"

"Roger, Commander. Just give me a moment to transfer the connection. You realize there will be some delay time in the comms?"

"Roger that, Captain." He sat back and waited. A timid voice interrupted his thoughts as his wife came on the air. "Jason," she sobbed his name, "I thought you were dead. They wouldn't tell me anything." Jason could hear the fire beginning to creep into her voice.

"I know, darling. Things were really nip and tuck up here for a while. We didn't know what was going to happen. It was natural that the General wouldn't want to get our hopes up needlessly. You of all people should understand that."

The line crackled as he waited for her to receive his transmission. "When are you coming home? We miss you and the kids need to see you."

Jason had to hold his hand over his mouth to contain the sob that burst out. He couldn't contain the tears as they flowed. He wanted to see them so badly – and knew the impossibility of that.

"Molly, this isn't going to be easy. For either of us. I'm on my way back to Mars. Just listen to me while I try to explain it." He rushed right on but not before he heard her response as it burst like a bubble through the comms channel. "They can't possibly do that!"

"We can't argue about this, Molly. We really can't. There is a job that has to be done and I'm the only one who can do it."

"Jason, that's bullcrap and you know it. Now tell me what is really going on. I can't stand it when you try to sugarcoat things. Don't keep the truth from me, please."

Jason and the General had gone over this very point earlier and O'Keefe had left it up to Jason to break the truth to his wife. They both agreed that they would rather not open up that can of worms, but Jason had known it would come to the point.

Molly could never dodge an issue. She had to approach things head on. After all, she was the wife of an astronaut. She had already crossed the bridge of knowing he could die. She just couldn't accept not knowing.

"Very well. Did the General fill you in on what happened on the way back from the Mission?"

"Yes, he told me some of it. Said a couple members of your crew were dead, but he wouldn't say how or why. What really happened up there?"

Jason sat back for a moment. Where to start? "I don't know how to really start this but will try to give you the condensed version and then you can ask questions after I finish." He jumped right in.

"Tony was killed on the surface and Marsella came down with a fungus in her lungs once we got the hatch closed and got back into orbit. We docked with the orbiter before the creatures emerged. They apparently were laying in wait for us and punched holes in Tony's and Marsella's suits. It took them a couple days to incubate inside my crew, but when they came out they were some nasty characters," he paused for a moment to let it sink in and to get his thoughts together.

"Molly, they did things to the rest of the crew and to me. The crew was placed inside their sleep chambers and infected. They used me to feed from. Seems they needed to have a fresh blood supply to make the transition from being Martian to being a cross between Martian and human. We have three of them on board now that we are taking back to Mars. They have nuclear devices strapped to their backs and are demanding that we help them when we get back to Mars orbit. I don't know what is going to happen when we get there."

"But you are coming back to us?" A plaintive plea was apparent in her voice, even across the distance separating them.

"I don't really know, Molly. Captain Baldwin and I stole the Pegasus with the intent of coming home, but events kept us from it. Now we have the mission to complete. After that, we'll have to see."

"Jason Martin, you aren't telling me the whole truth," her accusation scalded his face as he struggled with what he hadn't said.

"No, I guess you deserve to hear the rest from me. Molly, I can't come back to Earth. Now or ever. I'm one of them."

"I don't understand. One of them – what? What happened to you?"

"They infected me with their virus that made me like them. If I come anywhere near Earth millions of people will be infected with what I have. And you most definitely don't want that. Molly, these creatures are what we used to call the undead. Their evolution took a distinctly different turn from ours. When Mars lost its oceans the creatures had to adapt and become more like the sand of their planet. They are actually a virus that can be supported only with our blood. Some of their spoors made it to Earth during our early civilization. We knew them as blood-sucking vampires."

That sunk in. Molly's voice was subdued when she came back on line. "You really are serious, aren't you? You can't come back to us. You bastard! You promised me you would be back. What am I going to tell our children? That their daddy is a vampire and can't be seen with them anytime in their future? You unmitigating bastard!"

Jason let her have her say. He silently was relieved that she wasn't breaking down. That would happen later but for right now she was full of fire. "It isn't fair that you were put in harm's way like that. Jason, I want some heads over this. We need you!"

"I know you do, but I can't change what has happened. I've changed. I can no longer come anywhere near you. It wouldn't be fair to you or the children."

Molly took a turn that shocked him. "What about Captain Baldwin? Michelle, isn't it? Is she also infected? Are you two an item against the monsters? Jason, tell me the truth."

Jason hung his head for a moment. "She can't help it, Molly. Michelle became infected when I broke out of quarantine. She is now a hybrid like me. There is an attraction there but you know how people are under extreme pressure. But know for a fact that you will always remain in my heart."

"A fat lot of good that will do me. Go to her, Jason. Go to hell with her!"

"Molly, it doesn't have to be like this."

"What, it doesn't have to end like this? Is that what you're saying? That you want to have the best of both worlds? Your life long sweetheart on Earth and that enticing creature on Mars? You are a bastard. You couldn't even keep your promise to come back to me. I should have found this out sooner, Jason."

The connection broke off before he could reassure her. She had hung up. Jason reached over and was about to shut off the panel when Captain Wang's voice came through, "Do you want us to get her back for you, Commander?"

Jason shook his head. "No, I think we said everything that we're going to say. Let's just leave it there, shall we? Pegasus out." He hit the switch savagely and started to get up. Tony's hand forced him back into his chair.

"Now that was wholesome and fulfilling, wouldn't you say? The hero is now ready to give his life so his people can live like sheep. What do you think, Commander? That your way of life won't be changed completely by what you are going through? Let me give you a clue. Where I come from they are not going to welcome you with open arms. Especially when they see the mess you've brought back to them." He stepped back and sat in the copilot's chair.

"I heard enough of your conversation to know how you feel about me. So leave off with the storm clouds in your face, Commander. You see, I'm what you would consider a criminal on my own world. I thought I told you that before. Stop me if I did, but it's really going to be good to walk into the royal presence and know that I'm now in command and not some genetically altered personage. And you, Commander, are going to help me do just that. Otherwise, I give the high sign to my crew in the back and they proceed to feed upon your precious companion."

Jason started to rise and head for the back. "Let it go, Commander," Tony ordered. "Sit down or I'll tear her throat out myself. I don't have to have both of you, you know. In fact, I don't have to have either one of you."

"You do if you want to get anywhere near Mars." Jason pointed out at the cruisers they both could see. "Once an hour one of us has to report in to one of them. There is a specific rotation to the reporting that only Captain Baldwin and I know. I don't know her sequence and she doesn't know mine. They are under orders to open fire if that sequence is not followed, or if they think we've been tampered with. Is that clear?"

Tony regarded Jason for several heartbeats then nodded. "Crystal clear, Commander. I can't say I envy you the pressure of having to keep that up the entire trip. But, do have your fun." He arose smoothly and went into the back. Jason was going to follow when Michelle burst through the curtain and into his arms. She was terrified.

"They were going to eat me," she finally got out around the sobs that wracked her body. Jason could do very little but hold her close. Tony was right – it was going to be a long flight. A very long and trying flight. "Just stay away from them," he advised. "I've got your back."

They both sat and she opened the comms channel to check in. Afterwards she stared ahead at nothing. 'How did she take it?' she tight beamed to him.

'Not good. Not good at all. I'll fill you in later,' was all he would say.

25 A FRIENDSHIP OF SORTS

"What did she say?" Michelle timidly broached the subject. Jason had sat stiffly in the command chair for over an hour, talking to no one in particular, but going through the motions silently in his head. Some of those actions had played out in his features.

Michelle had tried to give him room to be alone with his inner thoughts but could not bring herself to leave the command cabin. No way was she going into the back without Jason with her. She would sleep in her chair if she had to.

Jason looked at her. 'She was very upset. I couldn't have expected otherwise, but I guess I kind of wanted her to be a little more understanding. I wanted too much.'

'No, you wanted what your heart wants. You wanted your family and they've been taken away from you. It isn't your fault, Jason. You didn't do this to them.' She jerked her thumb toward the rear of the craft. "They did it! Not you," she completed loudly.

Amanda stepped through the curtain onto the command deck. "Now don't let me be the one to interrupt your little love spat." She looked at Jason. "Bartam wants to speak with you."

Jason shrugged. "He knows where I am. Last I heard he grew two legs when he took over my crewmember's body. He can come to me."

Amanda leaned close. "Don't make this any harder than you must, Commander. I'm not going to hurt your little companion, if that's what you are afraid of," she leered at Michelle and licked her lips. "She does look good, huh?"

Jason's fist lashed out and he grabbed the front of Amanda's jumpsuit and pulled viciously. "You touch another member of my crew and there won't be any landing anywhere."

He was staring into Amanda's eyes, which were very near to his. She tried to push him back, but he came out of his chair and pinned her against the bulkhead. "No innuendoes, no threats, nothing! I'll tolerate nothing from any of you." He shoved hard and stormed toward the back.

Amanda breathed heavily and stepped toward Michelle who raised a stun pistol and pointed it directly at Amanda's head. "One more step and I'll fry that pretty face of yours. Believe me, I just want to watch you writhe."

"And set off a nuclear explosion in the process? I don't think so," she completed smugly, but her eyes betrayed the confusion she was feeling. She kept her face to Michelle as she backed past Jason who was now coming forward.

'What did he want?' she demanded after Amanda had left them.

'He wanted me to arrange a meal with the commanders of the other ships. Seems he thinks they will lose control if they don't have someone to feed upon during the trip. I told him nuclear fire would be preferable to allowing another human to be subjected to his form of torture.'

'Good for you,' she remarked with enthusiasm once more evident in her mental voice. 'Now tell me about Molly. I need to know her, even if it's just through your eyes. I want to know what I'm going to have to deal with. You understand that, don't you?'

Jason nodded. 'I know exactly what you are going through. Michelle, she was my high school sweetheart. I never knew anyone else. Didn't want to. She was to be the one who I grew old with. She has been everything to me for so many years now. How can I let all that go?'

"I'm not asking you to," she said aloud.

They sat silently communing until it was time for him to check in with the Argus. "I want to talk with the General again before we get too much further," he said to the Argus' commander, Captain Wilson. "This check-in schedule is going to get us all killed, but we still need to have a fail-safe method of ensuring we don't get taken over here."

Captain Wilson agreed. "Do you want me to run interference with him?" she asked.

"Only if you think you've come up with a plan you can live with. Otherwise, no belay that. Get in touch with him and from now on use the method I used to contact him the first time. He will feed you the information. Trust him, Captain. For the present let's continue with the present system of checking in."

"Roger, Commander. Wilson out."

The line went dead, leaving everyone on the Pegasus waiting for the next move to be played out. The tension was clear as Jason and Michelle heard Tony start throwing things against the bulkhead in the rear of the ship. Jason's smile was tight-lipped as he looked at Michelle. 'Let him stew on that for a while.'

'What did you just tell her to do?' she tight beamed.

'Can't say too much, but we will be given a break on checking in. O'Keefe will fill her in on the process. For right now you will continue to follow our verbal process. Bartam can't tap into this channel we're using without us knowing about his presence. And he doesn't know about the other method of communication that we are going to use. We just have to get things set up. Then I'll fill you in completely.'

Jason started to sit back and felt a nudge within his mind. It didn't feel like anything he had received from the three in the back, so he opened up. 'Who is there?'

'A friend. Commander, you are now in range where I can help you. But you have to let me.'

'Who are you?' Jason demanded.

'I would rather not say at this point. Suffice it to say that I'm no friend to those you are ferrying. Will you trust me?'

'We don't seem to have a choice, do we?' Jason noted that the person was also talking with Michelle at the same time.

'Yes, Commander. We are capable of setting up a comms channel between you and your people in the other probes. You can continue your ruse of checking in, but need only to do it to keep Bartam off-guard. If it's OK with you, I'll show you how to do it.'

'Why? Why do you want to help us?' Jason inquired the same question that he knew was on Michelle's mind.

'Just say I have reason to assist you. I don't want those devices that Bartam carries within parsecs of my planet. We need to work together with you, Commander. To ensure your well being as well as our own.'

'I understand, but I want to know who I'm dealing with.'

'Can't do that just yet,' the connection broke abruptly and Jason sat back. 'We might have a chance,' he whispered.

26 DECISION TIME FOR O'KEEFE

General Thomas J. O'Keefe looked back from the mirror at the civilian waiting, no, wanting to happen and shuddered. Half of his adult life had been spent in space or on the Moon. He had gotten overall command of Mars Mission III because of being passed over for the previous two missions.

Now he didn't know if he had the fortitude to conclude this one. Especially after the two-way conversation he had listened to between his premier pilot and that pilot's wife. It wasn't a scene he wanted to go through again, anytime soon, or ever.

Jason Martin had been like a son to him. He had given Molly away because her father had died the year before her wedding. She had come to him in tears one day and asked for the favor that he had felt privileged to receive.

She had done him an honor with her request. Now he had to meet her glare and know that he had something to do with her never being able to see her husband again. And also knowing that Jason wasn't physically dead – just very unavailable, and would be for the rest of their natural lives.

The General drew a shaking hand across his face and sighed deeply and sadly. There was nothing that he could have done differently. She didn't understand that if Jason had not made the decision he did that he would have had to give the order to have the Pegasus shot down.

He couldn't allow the virus infesting Jason and Michelle to reach Earth. That had been made plain to him, but she wouldn't be interested in that. She would ask him how he knew. Molly wanted answers and he didn't have a lot that he could give to her.

His reverie was broken by the chiming of a console that had been set up in the corner of his suite of living spaces/Officers quarters. He saw the amber light come on as the screen resolved itself into an older version of himself. At least that was how the old lady appeared to him. He felt most days now that they must be the same age.

"You will live many of your years before you even come close to being my age, General." Angat of Deneb spoke slowly and carefully. "I see our children are on their way back to a confrontation on Mars. They suspect nothing."

"No, they suspect nothing. Are you sure this is going to bring the Martians to the surface so you can take care of them?"

"There is a 97% probability of that, General." Angat paused, then continued, "Listen, old friend, we are no more pleased than you are of how this has worked out. If we had been in orbit at the time they were coming back, this wouldn't have been allowed. But we have to take advantage of this situation. You understand that it is only a matter of time before the Martians convince themselves that they have a right to invade your planet using the same methods that Bartam used. We can't allow that. Their society would do immense damage to yours."

"I understand it, but there are people down on the planet who don't. Most notably a young lady who doesn't understand why she can't see her husband again."

"Yes, we listened in on that conversation. We will try to do all we can to alleviate that situation when the time comes, but we may not even be able to reverse the process. It may be that we can take her to him, but that would be proliferating the situation. What we don't want is for further spread of the hybrids. We may have no choice but to terminate your people to save the rest of your civilization. I would certainly be saddened if we can't come up with a better solution."

"I know. I will also. Now, down to business. Have you found those you were seeking on our world?"

"Yes, we've found them. Fortunately, they are unable to travel far because of their aversion to sunlight. It burns their skin. Getting all of them will require a major operation and at the moment we don't think the possibilities are great that we can get them all. And that is a must. We have to break up their cells and get all of them. Nothing else is acceptable."

"How many humans do you estimate have been affected?"

"Nearly four hundred that we can identify. You see, the bloodline is running thin and these beasts think nothing of fighting among themselves for control of territory and bodies. Bartam would have infused them with new life. Within one of your life times at least half of your world would have been infected in some way. He had an extra large dose of infestation that he was going to unleash on you. You can't possibly measure the damage he would have caused."

The General sat on the edge of his chair. "Don't you think it's time that we go public with our leaders down on Earth?"

Angat shook her head sadly. "No, General, I don't. Some of our people give that option a slight positive chance of having a favorable effect, but I don't think so. Your people cannot be empowered if they think a superior race is out here looking out for them. You must do it on your own, without our help being apparent."

"But you are stepping in this time to help us. Why can't they know about it?"

"General, we are stepping in at this moment in time because it is critical that your people be given at least another one hundred years of unadulterated maturing before contact can be made that will be meaningful and helpful to you. You have to learn to venture to the stars on your own, without our assistance."

"I understand," the General sighed quietly. "What can I do now to carry my end of the load?"

"You can continue to direct the efforts of your people in the direction they are going. We have to allow Bartam to land, preferably crash land, upon the Martian surface. After that, events will take their turn and we will be able to insert people into critical situations where we can take care of this problem once and for all."

"You aren't talking about exterminating the Martians, are you?" he inquired softly.

"No, we don't feel we will have to do that. But we do have to cut back on the aggressive tendencies. We can do that by cutting off some of their higher echelon of personnel. Wish us all well in this undertaking, General. We may need it in the end."

"I do wish us well, Angat. General O'Keefe out." The General sat back and stared at the now blank screen for what seemed like ages. He had a definite job to do and it started with making sure an upset housewife had something to give her hope.

He only hoped for himself that he wasn't building up her hopes just to see them dashed. A lot was going to happen. A lot.

27 OBTAINING MARS' ORBIT

Mars loomed large in the view screen of the Pegasus. Michelle had butterflies in her stomach with each passing hour. She hadn't expected to ever come this close to another planet. She had been disappointed when General O'Keefe had selected her for his personal staff.

She wanted at least to make one trip as a crewmember on a mission. Now she was sitting as the co-pilot on a very critical mission. The General had made it plain that she had a job to do. Time was now approaching when she would need to perform her part.

She looked across the short distance separating herself from Commander Martin. She couldn't remember the first time she had felt so close to anyone. Nor could she remember how her life had been before he came into it. By storm.

'Yes, he took you by storm and you folded like a silly school girl to everything he wanted,' she thought silently within a private place that only she knew. 'He doesn't even realize how deeply I've fallen for him. But most of it is probably pheromones. I hope we get back from this. I'd love to run some analysis on the chemical balance of our bodies.'

Michelle's reverie was interrupted as Jason awoke and met her stare. "How long was I out?" he asked, scanning the command board in front of him.

"Not long enough. Less than three hours. Jason," she stopped for a moment to give him the chance to read the latest directive from the General. "We need to get you at least that much more rest before we make landfall. We've got at least twelve hours before we insert into Mars's orbit. Let me give you something that will help you rest."

Jason shook her off. "We don't have the luxury of that now. There's no way only one of us can handle Bartam's crew if he decides to pull something."

"Yes, but we have the Argos to give us backup. Jason, we really need you to be as fresh as you can be during our approach. I'm not that good as a pilot, but I do know my medical discipline and your tank is low. You've been running thin all flight. Now, I'm asking you to step down for a while and take something. Please. So we can count on you when we need you."

Her common sense seeped through. He had been running on empty for a while now. And his head felt it. Funny thing how he actually missed having the DocBot on board, but they were only being used for mission flights. He smiled at Michelle. "I guess it's a good thing that I broke into the office of a good medic, huh?"

She blushed and glanced back out to the horizon. Mars was coming up faster than she wanted it to.

She would much rather have had another couple weeks to assimilate all the changes the virus had made in each of them. Now that research was going to take a back seat to action. And once they were on the planet it would become a moot point. She suspected that survival was going to be on their minds.

Both were shocked to look around and see Amanda standing on the flight deck, looking out into space at her new planet. "How long have you been standing there?" Jason asked gruffly.

"Long enough to know that you should probably listen to your doctor. You always did have a problem listening, you know that?" Her yellow-green eyes disturbed Jason as she looked deeply into his soul. "Yes, everyone on board will be counting on you to get us down safely."

"I'll take it under advisement. Right now I need to concentrate on setting up that approach, so if you'll excuse me." He left the statement hanging in the air between them and began passing coordinates to Michelle's astrogation console.

Amanda looked at the back of their heads and felt a sadness. She had trained intensively to go into space with Commander Martin. She had responded instantly to every directive he gave up to the point when she came out of stasis to find that she had changed.

Changed forever from all appearances. Bartam had pointed out some of the not so subtle changes that the virus had done on the human physiology. The water level had been significantly reduced in their new bodies. Organs were more solidified and became more shock proof. The entire blood flow system had undergone changes that she found mysterious even now. But she still had the same soul, or thought she did. It was ruled by the body, but she felt it was still there somewhere.

She stepped back into the cargo bay and stopped Tony from moving forward. "There is nothing to be gained by getting his blood pressure up." She looked deeply into Tony's eyes and saw that he really didn't care what she thought, but stood her ground. He finally shrugged and turned around.

His mind seemed preoccupied on what was going to happen when they finally arrived on the planet. She watched his back and realized how much she hated the fact that there even had to be a confrontation at all.

Jason received the coordinates back from the Argos that he had requested and plotted them into his console. He needed to know where each of the cruisers was going to set up station keeping. The Argos commander had placed her ship directly behind him. Somehow he felt a comfort in knowing that they were back there.

Finally things were set up to his satisfaction. He turned to Michelle and said, "Well, doc. I've done about all I can do to get us there safely. I'll take whatever you say, but as tired as my mind feels, I don't think

I'll need anything. Besides, how do you know that whatever you would have given Jason the human will have the same impact on Jason the thing?"

They both laughed and she shook her head. "I don't know that anything will work with what we have become. I'll monitor your patterns for a while and administer something if you don't achieve REM. Agreed?"

"Roger, you're the doctor on this trip." His mind snapped back to when he had said something similar to another crewmember. He sadly shook his head as he slipped the glove on that would monitor his physical well being. Jason had barely closed his eyes before he slipped into sleep. Michelle monitored his vital signs and sat back, waiting for the hammer to fall.

28 CRASH LANDING

The Argos commander powered up her forward blasters and awaited the orders she knew were coming. Her second in command, Captain Ben Davis, raised his eyebrows and silently questioned the action. "General's orders," was all she would say. He let it go at that and they waited.

Aboard the Pegasus, the tension was rising. Tony had come forward but was stopped at the flight deck partition by Michelle. "I could throw you through the bulkhead behind you. How dare you even try to stand in my way?" he growled at her.

She stood her ground. "Nothing is going to awake Commander Martin until I say so and I don't care what you think about it." She held up a little home-crafted, hand-held device and showed him the switch she had installed on it. "Two can play your little game."

"You don't scare me," he said, but backed up a step.

"Let me make things crystal clear for you," she took the initiative and discovered she liked it. "The General said to deliver you to Mars. He didn't say you had to be in any shape to be sociable. In fact, he would probably appreciate it more if you rained down in pieces from orbit. So get back and leave both of us alone."

Tony sneered as he took another step toward the rear of the craft. "You haven't won yet. You know that. You humans want to hold onto life as long as you can. Waiting for your Lone Ranger to save you. Yes, I've done some research on your culture. You're always getting yourself into situations where you need to be rescued."

"At least the Lone Ranger helped the less fortunate. Did you miss that? Or is it possible there is no humanity left in you, that you can't feel anything for anyone? Not even for your own people."

"They are of no concern to you. Just drop us off at the curb and we'll take it from there. Now get in there and get your pilot off his tail and us on the ground. Destiny awaits." With that Tony turned on his heels and sauntered away, leaving Michelle fuming that he had gotten the last word in.

She stared for a moment at his back disappearing into the crew's living quarters, then turned back to the front. Jason was scheduled to awaken in about twenty minutes.

She laid the dummy device on the console in front of her and started setting up the procedure that she, the General, and the Argos commander had painstakingly put together. They had to time it right and were counting on Tony to control his crew through the ensuing chaos.

They were heavily counting on Bartam's need for revenge. Michelle thought they might be placing too much emphasis on that point, but couldn't convince anyone else that she had insight into the creature. And she could see their point. She was still acting out of fear, abject fear, of being at the mercy of those creatures in the back.

On the Argos a lamp lit on the Commander's console. Her eyes hovered immediately above it, as if even now she didn't want her mind to accept that the countdown had begun that would plunge the Pegasus out of control into the thin atmosphere of Mars. She had to get the shot just right. It had to disable the craft without destroying the livability of its occupants. Her hands shook as she brought the Argos directly behind her quarry.

Ben Davis noted the shake in the navigation system and looked expectantly in her direction. "Can I give you a hand with something,

Commander?"

"No, Ben. This is something I have to take care of myself." Her resolve and hands calmed as she lined up the blaster point on the aft nacelle of the Pegasus. She waited for the amber light to extinguish and go to green. They had been concerned that there be little, if any, indication that something was going to take place until after it happened. She was waiting now for Captain Baldwin.

On the Pegasus, Jason Martin came awake and sat upright. His eyes did what they always did when he returned to consciousness – surveyed the board in front of him for anything out of the ordinary. His board was green but his eyes settled on the makeshift device that Michelle had left on her console.

"What is that for?" He pointed to it as Michelle jumped at the sound of his voice.

She stammered, trying to bring her heart back into control. "It's just something I made up to give Bartam something to think about while you were asleep." She picked it up and turned it over in her hand. "He was insisting on disturbing you and I figured I'd just call his bluff." Her voice sounded kind of lame to her, but Jason appeared to have bought her explanation.

"And he accepted that?"

"Well, he went into the back and I haven't seen him since." She pressed the button and a corresponding light turned green on the Argos. The Pegasus lurched suddenly as the beam from the blaster sheared the ion exhaust pod from its rear. The Pegasus went into a skid and slid around sideways to the planet. Captain Wilson re-sighted the blaster and clipped about six feet off the starboard wing as the Pegasus came around. The craft tumbled deeper into the thin atmosphere of Mars.

Jason stared wide-eyed at Michelle in the moment of impact. 'We were meant to ride this one in, weren't we?' he tight-beamed to her.

She only nodded. At the moment she didn't know how much

could be intercepted by Bartam. Jason would have to trust her. Her eyes said as much when his met hers. He knew and nodded in return before returning his attention to the now useless controls. He began to fight with them as Tony rushed onto the flight deck.

"What the hell happened?" he demanded, trying to look through the windows of the cabin to gain some point of reference. "If your people are screwing with me, they will regret it! This device will be set off if I lose consciousness. Remember that!"

Jason didn't look at him. He had just seen the wing tip of the Pegasus spin off into space and understood the impact they were going to make when they went into the Martian landscape. There was no way that he was going to guide the bus into a smooth landing. He doubted that he could gain enough control to give them time to bail out.

"Captain Baldwin, get everyone into the high altitude suits and ensure they have braking devices. We are going to have about twenty minutes max before we reach altitude where we can use the ejection tubes. That is if they haven't been damaged. Check it out."

"Aye, sir," she responded and grabbed handholds as she went past Tony, who was trying to hold on to the bulkhead in spite of the pitch and yaw of the spacecraft. Jason looked back at Tony and growled, "You better get your ass back there with her. It's going to take all the time we have to get everyone into the suits." He moved past Tony into the back and started his own procedures to get ready to disembark.

Michelle caught his attention. "One of the tubes is blocked with jagged metal but the other one is in working order. When we will be in range to begin evacuation?"

Jason glanced at his watch. "Ten minutes to first exit." He looked around and saw that Buzz was almost ready to fasten his outer shell. "We need to have some atmosphere before we can go. Otherwise we will achieve too high a velocity for anything to stop us."

Buzz nodded and let Amanda check his connections. She finished, then patted him on the back and he moved toward the exit tube. Everyone else continued their prep as the time was counted down.

Michelle hit the button just as a thought occurred to her. She started to shout to Jason, then changed to thought control instead. 'How are we going to know which way this tube is pointing? We could be sending one of us into space. This tube packs quite a kick.'

Jason maneuvered toward the only porthole on his side of the ship and gestured for Amanda to get into the tube. "Go on my mark. We're going to have to hope that this bucket doesn't pitch too violently from your kick. I think we'll be able to compensate for it."

Michelle hit the button on his mark and Amanda shot off toward the planet. He saw her arms open wide to catch all the air she could as a brake. He motioned for Tony to enter the tube, but he hesitated.

His thought was very much present in Jason's mind. 'Don't worry. I will find you down there and if your people try to land, I will take some of them with me. Got that?'

'I'll see if I can wait for you on the surface,' he promised. Why should I try to find my way in when you can take me in – he continued in his own mind. He looked out the porthole and indicated to Michelle to hit the switch. Bartam was on his way back to the surface.

Jason smiled at Michelle and indicated she was to enter the tube. He waited until he was sure their craft was pointed in the right way, then hit the switch. A soft chuff was heard as she exited the tube, then Jason staggered across the room as something slammed into the back of the disabled vehicle. He went down to his knees and noticed the buckle that had appeared in the middle of the tube. He tried the vacuum mechanism and it was silent.

"Shit! This definitely isn't good," he said to himself. Jason stumbled forward and pitched onto the flight deck as the Pegasus turned onto its nose and rolled over. Hand over hand he worked his way into the command chair and strapped himself in.

His head hit the command console as the atmosphere became more dense and the nose bit in. Stars appeared before his eyes and he felt a knot raising in the middle of his forehead, inside his helmet. He blinked back the tears and tried to concentrate on figuring out if his face shield was busted. He didn't think so.

Very little time was left. Michelle was still at two thousand feet when she saw the Pegasus skid across the sand and finally dig itself into the dunes. She held her breath and waited. There was no explosion, so he might still be alive. She angled her descent in the direction of where the ship went in, but knew that he had crashed too far away for her to reach him on the fly.

Her complicity in the demise of the Pegasus suddenly hit her hard as she tried to fly her canopy in his direction. A knot that had developed long before entry into Mars' orbit suddenly burst and she could no longer hold back the tears. She was crying as her feet hit the sand and she rolled forward to take the shock. Her head was already raised in the direction of the crash as she tried to no avail to reach him on their mind link.

Michelle was on her feet and heading for the crash site when she was surrounded by long-armed, bipedal beings carrying long staves, which they pointed at her. One of them separated from the rest and bowed its head in her direction. 'Please to follow us. We mean you no harm, but must insist you come with us.'

'But I must rescue my friend and make sure he is OK,' she protested, but the circle around her didn't budge.

'Your friend will be well taken care of. Don't worry about him. You come with us.'

Michelle looked longingly in the direction of where she knew the Pegasus had gone down and tried in vain again to reach Jason on their internal link. It was silent. Not even the crackle and pop of space. Nothing. She shivered and turned to follow her captors.

29 "HE'S NOT IN THE PROBE"

"Your Majesty. He is not in the probe."

King Leopold's head snapped up and his gaze drilled through Amadeus, his advisor. "How can he not be there? Did your people arrive at the crash site right after the probe went in?"

"Yes, your Grace, they did. He could not possibly have gotten out of there without us seeing him. And he didn't eject from the capsule during flight. We are combing the area now for indications of what may have happened."

"You are certain he is not with Bartam's group? They aren't hiding him in some way, are they?"

Amadeus shook his head so hard his topknot quivered. "No, Sire. Two of those who picked up the survivors are in life debt to me to report back everything they see and hear. There is no way he can be amongst them."

Leopold considered for a moment that turned into minutes. "Amadeus, what was the condition of the command module of the probe?"

"Severely damaged and buried where it went into the dunes. But we've removed enough of the sand to know that he isn't there. We do have his companion, though."

The King's eyes narrowed. "She may have to do if we can't find the other one. I really wanted a full work-up on the male so our scientists could see if maybe Bartam was onto something when he merged with them. He may have inadvertently happened upon a way to extend our life cycles without us having to go through stasis all the time." His mind seemed a million miles away as he dismissed Amadeus. "Find him and bring the woman into my presence when they arrive."

"Yes, your Majesty. What do you want us to do with Bartam?"

"They are still wearing the explosive devices?"

"Yes, Sire."

"Have we successfully come up with a duplicate of their containment devices? Can we contain them?"

"The answer is a conservative yes. As long as we can keep the three of them separated we can be reasonably assured of containment. I've taken steps to ensure that happens when they arrive within the walls. They will be separated."

"Good," Leopold looked into his advisor's eyes. "We can't afford to blow this one, Amadeus."

Amadeus lowered his eyes and nodded. "We will not."

About twenty kilometers away Michelle Baldwin was starting to flag. They had been walking steadily since the Pegasus' crash. The beings guarding them had much longer legs and she was finding it difficult keeping up. The two bringing up the rear were getting fed up with pushing her forward. She could tell from their facial features that they considered her to be inferior to themselves.

Buzz fell back into step with her as twilight suddenly fell on them. His breath froze almost immediately as the temperature fell dramatically. "Have you been able to establish any link with Commander Martin?" he asked her.

"No. I haven't felt anything from him since he went forward after the exit tube was damaged," she looked sharply at him. "Why are you so concerned with Jason?"

"He used to be a crewmate of mine," he said, not looking at her. "I still have somewhat of humanity remaining in me. You may not think it, but I do owe the Commander for saving my life. That is not an easy debt to owe, nor repay."

He finally turned toward her. "Let's just say I owe him and wouldn't have contributed to harming you on the Pegasus earlier. I had to go along with Bartam to make it look good. You do understand that, don't you?" The last part was spoken so low that she almost didn't hear it.

"But you held me down for the others," she started to protest, then stopped herself as she saw the sincerity in his eyes.

"I would not have allowed them to harm you," he said and turned in the direction that the group was going. "We are both going to need a friend when we get inside."

"What do you mean by that?" she inquired after several heartbeats had passed.

Buzz glanced sideways and said so softly she almost lost his words again, "The local government is going to want to know what changes have taken place within our bodies after the virus did its trick. I'd be surprised if we aren't put through some severe tests once we get inside. Their scientists are going to want some answers. Just try to cooperate with them wherever possible. I'll try to keep you close to me for Jason's sake. Man, I wish he had made it out of that thing with us."

He looked back toward the crash site and shrugged. There wasn't much anyone could do for Jason now.

Michelle glanced back over her shoulder with him and was struck by the amount of pent up grief and emotion that suddenly boiled to the surface. She hadn't realized before or maybe just hadn't had the luxury of thinking about it, but she really had fallen head over heels in love with the guy.

Tears froze on her cheeks as she tried to look through the distance to find him. He wasn't there. She bowed her head and shuffled forward, suddenly more tired than she had ever been.

In the front of the column Bartam was cursing under his breath at Amanda. "What do I have to do to get some respect around here? You'd think that we are prisoners, instead of conquering heroes. Don't these fools realize I could snuff out their miserable existence in a heartbeat?"

Amanda had been listening to him for longer than she cared to. "Just give it a rest, why don't you? Whoever is in charge obviously chose people they could trust or they wouldn't be out here at all. These are the mindless ones. They follow orders, they don't think. Now be quiet so I can get some thinking done before we get inside. Our future might depend on it."

She walked on past him and left Bartam standing by himself. She didn't know how close to the edge of insanity he was, but figured that it was close. Somehow, she was going to have to control the situation that was coming up and she really didn't feel up to it. It was obvious, though, that Bartam wasn't going to do anything but bluster and get them killed. She couldn't allow that.

30 ENEMY'S TREATY

The prisoners were pretty flagged out by the time they arrived at what appeared as just a shallow indentation in the sand dunes before them. Michelle tried to estimate how long they had been traveling but her mind was too fuzzy to allow her any clear indications. 'I don't think I've ever been this tired. Not even during basic training.'

'And you probably won't get a chance once we get inside to rest.' Michelle looked up to see Amanda staring back at her. She fell in step as they both went down into the depression that closed in around them.

They had to turn sideways to squeeze through the passageway. It was tall enough, just a little cramped. Looking at their captors she realized why. They were at least seven feet tall. The LA Lakers would probably want any one of them just for their height.

Michelle sighed and tried to concentrate on the task of getting through the corridor. She was beginning to get claustrophobic when the passageway opened up into a loading platform for a railway device.

A flat carriage on wheels, with no sides nor seats occupied a set of rusty rails in front of the group. Their captors pushed them toward it and indicated they should get on. Michelle sat between Amanda and Buzz. After looking at the expression on Bartam's face, she wanted to get as far from him as possible.

Amanda must have sensed what she was thinking. 'Just stick close to me and Buzz. We will try to disarm the situation when we get into the inner chambers. Listen to me.' She had to shake Michelle to get her fully awake. 'We don't know what they have in mind for us. We do know that they are curious about how we assimilated your bodies and about your technology. So we do have some bargaining power, but probably not much.'

She paused as their captors began pushing their transportation.

Wheels squealed on axles long overdue for maintenance, but the railway car started to move under the brute strength being applied to it. Everyone on board sat quietly involved in their own thoughts. Michelle kept fading in and out as sleep tried to fully engulf her.

She never did know just how long it took for them to arrive at the end of the line. They were physically dragged off the platform and taken into separate rooms.

Amadeus carefully observed the transfer of prisoners into their holding cells. He was clearly amazed that Bartam's process had worked. His own scientists had discounted, during the first expedition that had landed on Mars, that they could possibly make any use out of the water-laden carcasses of the Earthmen. He hadn't even considered any techniques that would reconstitute the beings into something more closely resembling their own.

"You need to see this," one of his staff called his attention to the results of a scan he had just completed. "By the sacred pools. She is still over 75% water. We could transport their people here just for the water alone and make a fortune."

Amadeus considered the figures. "Why didn't we consider this when they came the first time?" His rough eyebrows raised and the fellow slunk backwards.

"We just didn't think of it," he began, nervously.

"And the King is going to have someone's head because you didn't think of it," he paused at the one-way wall and considered the impact that statement was going to have upon Leopold. It wasn't something to lead off a conversation with, for sure.

"Raise the temperature in there and see how she fares. I want sonograms every five degrees. We have to know how they react to extremes. And keep me posted on the others, as well."

His staff hurried to do his bidding. He considered for a moment an aspect of their society that had bothered him for many cycles now. The comment earlier had triggered thoughts he didn't really want to consider, but must.

He had to find a way of keeping his brightest minds from going into stasis. They seemed to lose everything they had been working on prior to regeneration. It was almost as if they couldn't carry their combined knowledge with them through the process. He had to spend so much time downloading data so they could relearn to the point where they were. And by the time he got them there – it was time for them to return to the chamber.

'We need to prolong the cycle and these Earthlings are the key to the process. I'm sure of that. Maybe not in the same way that Bartam was going to use them, but we will use them all the same. They have now delivered the transportation devices to us. After we determine how to use them, we will set up a constant supply of water from their planet to ours. We can go in the luxury holiday business, siphon a gallon or two while they're here enjoying the sights, and they will be none the wiser. According to these figures, humans lose a lot of their internal water every day…' his thoughts were interrupted.

"Minister. You need to come quickly. Bartam is demanding an immediate audience with the King and says he will explode his device if we don't comply."

Amadeus arose and followed his servant. They didn't have far to go to reach the cell where Bartam was being incarcerated. He stood as Amadeus entered the cell but didn't bother to bow his head.

"I want to see whichever stick figure you have behind the throne and I want to see it now," he caustically remarked as the door shut behind Amadeus.

"That stick figure is King Leopold and he isn't the nobody you may want to think. I'll determine, first of all, when we are ready to have an audience with anyone. Then the King will determine how much longer your miserable existence is going to continue." He looked Bartam straight in the eyes though he had to stoop slightly to accomplish that task. "You are in no position to even request an audience."

Bartam walked around Amadeus, all the while keeping their eyes locked. The older man was disconcerted by the maneuver but tolerated it. "What makes you so certain that I can't do exactly what I said when we arrived? You obviously noted the explosion we set off on their moon. That was done to give you notice that the same can be done here. You can't control it or me. This precious city of yours will be glassy and radioactive for many cycles."

Amadeus stepped back and smiled. "This hovel is of no consequence. We have moved the government to other locations during the time it took you to make the transit from the Third Planet. There is nothing that you can harm. Besides, we are now able to use your methods and will contain the blast you've so highly touted."

Bartam's eyes narrowed. Something didn't exactly ring true. "If that were so, we would already be dead, so, dear Amadeus, you aren't playing with someone you can just slough off and forget. Remember, there are three devices. You can't possibly contain all of them. Someone is going to die."

"Yes, I'm afraid you are right. Someone is going to die and His Majesty has decreed that you will be the one. He can't abide the stench of you up his royal nostrils any more. And you'll notice that we have been careful to keep you and your companions separated. You might all three set off the devices and you might do it in unison, but I doubt that even you have the stomach for so noble a gesture."

His statement kind of hung in the air between them. "Are you seeking to make a deal with me?" Bartam inquired, almost too surprised by the prospect to get the words out.

"Perhaps. That depends on how cooperative you're prepared to be."

Bartam returned to the drop down seating along the wall, sat down and looked back at his newfound friend. "What exactly do you want from us?"

Amadeus shook his head. "Not the three of you. Just you. The others must pay for your crimes against the state. Call it the price of loyalty to a cause, if you like."

"And how is the King going to be placated, knowing that I'm still alive?"

Amadeus sat down before he answered. "He won't know. We will inform his Majesty that all three devices were detonated and that you were consumed by the fire. He won't like that because he is so looking forward to removing your head from your shoulders in a personal way."

Bartam shortened his neck as he thought of the King's claws passing through his body. He had seen it done several times. They all had. He wasn't interested in having the procedure done to him.

"So my new friends are to be sacrificed. What about the Earthling we brought in with us? What becomes of her?"

"She has already been removed to another location. At the King's request, no less. She will be used for many a test for many a cycle before we finally have all the information we need about them. In the meantime, you can provide us with hard data on how and where to strike to obtain the materials we need."

"So you are convinced, as I was, that our destiny lies on the Third planet?"

"No. I'm not convinced of that at all. We weren't made to take their bodies as our own. But we were made to take their resources."

"But you're really missing the point," Bartam argued. "We, you and I, can be kings in our own right. We can rule that world."

Bartam's words exploded from his head as Amadeus slammed him back into the wall. He barely had time between seeing stars to realize that the other's claws had encircled his throat. "You will play this my way, Bartam, or not at all!" Amadeus growled and started to squeeze.

"You forget the bomb!" Bartam screamed. Amadeus suddenly relaxed his grip.

"You tear my head off and this thing explodes. Someone else will pick up the pieces of advising the King."

Amadeus released his grip and stood up. "You need to decide how you are going to best serve me, Bartam. I will take no more grandiose ideas from you. We have to be practical and we have very little time left to act. Are you with me or not?"

Bartam considered for so long that Amadeus was afraid he was going to say no, but he finally nodded. "Yes, I will join your merry little conspiracy under one condition."

"Name it."

"I get to kill Leopold myself."

31 TIME FOR DEATH

Michelle awoke slowly. She had been through a lot since coming to Mars. Systematic probing, prodding, heating and cooling, sleep deprivation and other sordid experiments had been performed. She raised herself on her arms and looked around her new quarters.

Sparse wasn't the word. The only thing in the room besides her was a stone pedestal that looked as if it might have been used as a very hard bed. She woke several feet away from it where she had been dumped the previous night.

Three guards had come into the room where she was being held for testing and indicated she was to follow them. Her watch had been removed early on so she had no idea of how much time had passed since they arrived on Mars.

She followed her guards as they squeezed through various underground tunnels. Her legs finally gave out on her and they ended up dragging her between them the rest of the way. Michelle felt her upper arms and winced. They hadn't been kind in their handling of her.

'I need to get out of here,' she thought as she looked around her. There was one thing that was very much missing in this cell. There was no water anywhere. In the other cell there had been a tall flask standing in the corner. There wasn't one here and she got the feeling that her present confinement was not going to be retrofitted with one.

Her mouth suddenly seemed as if it were full of cotton. She licked her lips and tried to forget the thirst that was already causing no small amount of discomfort. She set about trying to find a way out.

Meanwhile, Amanda and Buzz were busy passing information back and forth between their cells. Like Michelle's, their cells had no amenities. They had figured they had spent about eight days since their arrival and no one had come into their cells. They were clearly being ignored. 'I'm sure they are monitoring every move we make,' she sent to Buzz.

'Yeah, but question is – where is our fearless leader in all this? I haven't felt him anywhere for the past couple days. It's almost like he ceased to exist, but we both know that didn't happen.'

'I know,' she agreed with him and wondered again what was going on. 'Buzz, I think we've been had,' she said on a channel she was certain only the two of them shared. 'What is it that they are wanting us to do?'

'Die,' he stated flatly. 'I think we are the proverbial scapegoats. Bartam has been offered his freedom for whatever information about the humans he possesses and we are going to die to satisfy the indignation of the present rulers. Is that chilling enough?'

Amanda shuddered. 'Indeed. It is chilling and I'm not liking it one bit. I wonder what they are anticipating – are we supposed to go berserk and set off the bombs we're carrying?'

'I don't know, but if I don't get some water soon it may be a moot point. I'm not going on much further without.' Amanda could hear the weariness and boredom in his tone and nearly panicked as a thought hit her.

'That is exactly what they want!' she almost shouted aloud as the realization struck home. 'We are meant to go out in a series of explosions. Buzz, listen to me. Can you sense how close we are to each other?'

He was silent for some time but she could almost feel his thoughts. Finally, 'We are in cells right beside each other,' he said. 'And I located Bartam's device. It is in a closet between us. Amanda, they intend for us to fry and for that little bastard to go free. I'll tear his throat out myself!'

'Careful, my friend,' she advised. 'We need to conserve our energies for waiting them out. Can you get to his device?'

'I'm already ahead of you on that score,' he said. She waited while he investigated their situation.

'I've got it,' he stated.

'Has it been tampered with in any way?' she asked.

'Yeah, the timing mechanism has been removed. The only thing that will set it off now is proximity. When ours goes off...' he didn't have to finish his statement.

Amanda was silent for so long he thought she might not have heard him. 'Are you still with me?' he asked.

Yes, I'm still here. Just trying to see if anyone is around. I feel no cycles from anyone. Is there any kind of remote trigger on Bartam's device? We need to know if we can get out of here without setting it off.'

Buzz turned the pack over and looked all around it. 'Unless it has been placed inside the device. No. I can't find anything like that. What do you have in mind?'

'Well, we can't stay here. This place is a ghost town. Everyone has been moved out. Have you seen any remote monitoring devices except for the two-way mirrors in the walls?'

'No, I don't think they have that kind of technology. There is a lot of ground that they are going to have catch up to be any kind of threat to the Earth.'

'I agree. It appears that we can move around freely as long as we take all three of the packages with us. We need to get out of here.'

'I'm with you. Can you suggest something on these doors?' He was looking for a way to open his from the inside.

'Well, I think we are going to have to use some of that mental control we have and see if we can levitate things. Give me a moment to see what I can do.'

Buzz waited. He had no idea how she was going to accomplish what she had just said, but believed enough in his crewmate's abilities to wait patiently. He had almost given up on her though when an excited thought shot across their link.

'Got it! I'm at your door right now.' His door receded into the sandstone wall as she spoke. They hugged as he started to dart out the door. 'Get the device.' He returned and scooped it up. They headed down the passageway toward the outside.

Amadeus looked up as his assistant came into the room. "They are on the move. She figured out how to get out. We are still investigating that,' he was out of breath as he delivered the message. Amadeus smiled. Things were going exactly as he had thought they would.

He sat back and considered his next move. "Keep an eye on them and ensure they don't suspect they are being watched." His aide left the room and Amadeus smiled again. This was going to work to his advantage.

He pressed a stud in the desk in front of him. A moment later another assistant appeared at the door. Without looking up, he gave instructions for Bartam to be brought in.

Bartam couldn't help but think that he had somehow been had in all the machinations going on behind the scenes. He didn't trust Amadeus, but couldn't figure out a way to bypass him.

There was no one else who he could turn to. King Leopold was the only one with more power than Amadeus and Bartam knew how long he would last with him. 'Not long,' he admitted.

He walked into Amadeus' suite of offices and noticed the amenities that were the obvious trappings of being nearly royalty. "You wanted to see me?"

Amadeus looked up. "Yes. Your friends have escaped and have taken your device with them. What could they possibly want with it?' his eyes bored into Bartam's.

"I don't know. You said all the controls had been removed from it. They can't possibly control it without them," he considered the situation for a moment. "Maybe they think they have to take it with them or risk the possibility that it will go off prematurely if they leave the area."

Amadeus chuckled. "We thought about doing that. We are monitoring their progress. Did you know that they can manipulate their environment using thought control? Do other humans have that ability?"

Bartam shook his head. "No. I wasn't aware that any of them did. I saw no indication of it from any of them. What makes you think that?"

"The female opened her cell with the power of her mind. That's what gave it away. These humans are certainly resourceful. We are being amazed by them all the time. The other female has also held up far better than we expected. We are trying to see how long she can go without water now. Maybe she too will show some of this resourcefulness under duress. What do you think?"

"I don't know what to think," Bartam countered.

Amadeus sat back and placed his long arms behind his head. He looked long at Bartam before he finally asked, "You still don't trust me, do you, Bartam?"

Bartam shook his head. "No, can't say that I do. I'm not sure what it is that you want from me. I would have allowed old Leopold his satisfaction a long time ago." He looked straight at Amadeus. "What do you really want?"

"I want to solve some long term problems that we've had." Amadeus stood up and walked around behind his desk. "You are aware of how debilitating our dependence upon stasis is on us?"

Bartam nodded and waited for Amadeus to continue.

"We can barely hold ourselves together from one generation to the next. And things are getting progressively worse all the time. Within five cycles we will not have a candidate for the throne who will be able to lead us in any effective way," he paused for the full measure of his statement to sink in. Even in the foreign body he could see the impact on Bartam.

"Yes, we are dying as a people. I predict that we won't last another hundred cycles. As feral beings, maybe, but not as a civilization. I'm determined to take steps to counteract that. Now do you understand what I want with you? You have firsthand knowledge of the creatures who may be our salvation."

"But why should you care? You will go into stasis soon and will practically forget all about it. Someone else will take up the task of advisor."

"Yes, I will and they will. But we don't have the luxury anymore of allowing that to happen. Can't you suspend your anti-social feelings for long enough to realize that we are in serious trouble?"

Bartam shook his head and approached the other man. "We can still follow my plan and won't have to worry about cycles anymore. That is where we should be going."

"And the humans are going to allow that?"

That stopped Bartam in his tracks. He thought for a moment about what they had been through. "No. They are very methodical in protecting themselves."

"Exactly. We saw the way they deep freezed you on your way to their moon. They were indeed very methodical and have been since their first mission here. I think they knew about us then. That's why they sent a manned mission. Their physical units are able to store much more information than their mechanical ones. We sadly underestimated them."

Both stood silent and considered their next moves. Bartam spoke first. "There is no way that we can get anywhere near their world now. What is your plan?"

Amadeus smiled. "We have to provide them with reasons to come here. They are really big into tourism and will probably pay to come here to look around the sites of antiquity that we will build for them."

"You can't be serious," Bartam was clearly shocked by the underhanded straightforward approach the other was proposing.

"It is the only way that we can get what we want."

Bartam was clearly unconvinced. "They won't allow that. We have shocked their sensibilities to the point where it will be a long time before they allow us any type of commerce with them."

"I've been studying them closely. I think we can set up a conference with them and both walk away winners."

"Then you might want to think twice about those nuclear devices that are walking around out there," Bartam stated flatly.

"Yes, I agree. We need to let them get as far away as possible."

Bartam became animated again. "No, we don't. You don't understand the principles involved here. There is something called radioactive fallout that you have to consider. It mixes with sand and will get into what little atmosphere we have. Winds will drop it on our doorsteps and we will become sicker than you think. Amanda did a lot of research on the effects while we were in prison on their moon. Something called fallout will be with us for many cycles.

You can't allow that part of your plan to come about. That part must be reconsidered."

The desert spread out around them as Amanda and Buzz trekked toward the spot where the Pegasus had gone in. Amanda was still not convinced that they were alone nor that they were out of danger. She said as much to Buzz. "We have been had. You know that, don't you?"

Not breaking stride he nodded. "Yes, I've been giving it a lot of thought. How far away can we get from these devices and still maintain enough control over them to keep them from going off?"

"Not far enough to matter," she replied. They walked in silence from then on, each in their own world of confused thoughts.

32 REVELATION TIME

"Commander Martin, it's good to see you're awake," Arnak stood in the door as Jason turned around from examining one of the paintings on the wall. He hadn't heard the being come up nor the door open.

"I've come to take you to Angat," it said. Jason couldn't determine the sex of the being. The silver, non-descript clothing hung limply from straight shoulders.

"What are you?" he wanted to know.

"Angat will explain everything to you in due time. Will you follow me?" she turned and left. Jason hurried across the room, almost afraid that the door would suddenly disappear. He could swear it wasn't there before the being had appeared.

Jason fell in step beside the being and looked out the side of his eyes at what he finally determined must be a female of some species. "How did I get here?" he asked.

She didn't answer and her manicured eyebrows seemed to come together – possibly indicating that she had closed her receptor ports. Jason sighed. One question and he already had the feeling that he was going to get nothing from her.

Fortunately the passageway turned out to be short. Arnak stood before a door that Jason hadn't seen prior to her stopping. She announced him and stepped aside. Jason stepped into a room that seemed to be a nerve center for a spaceship.

There were several large screens covering the walls across from his entrance. Another being, this one ancient by anyone's standards, looked up from a seat in front of one of them. Her head swiveled around as Jason entered the room.

"Commander, I'm so glad you returned to us," she stood as he approached. "Let me introduce myself. I'm Angat of Deneb. We are the bogeyman Bartam told you about. Sit with me while I explain things to you. I know you've a lot of questions, so bear with me."

Jason sat across from her, crossed his legs and waited. Angat got right to the point. "You're wondering how you came to be here."

He nodded and she continued, "We have a teleportation device and lifted you out of the crash as it happened. Your General O'Keefe wouldn't have forgiven me if I'd let you get mangled."

She had his full attention. "What does the General have to do with things?" he inquired.

Angat waved her hand at the nearest wall screen that showed the surface of Mars up close. "There is where your ship went into the sand. You can still see it from space," she sighed.

"Yes, Commander, I know I didn't answer your question. Your General is the only person of your world beside you who is aware of our existence. We had to solicit his aid to ensure we had a high enough probability of success on this mission to warrant undertaking it."

Jason frowned. "What exactly is your mission?"

Angat paused for a moment. "How much do you know of the history of your world, Jason?"

"Very little that makes actual sense. I was brought up to believe in the God of our Bible and that we were placed on Earth to worship him. I've always suspected that the religious people of my world didn't have all the facts. And seeing you reminds me of why I thought that."

She nodded and placed her hands on her knees. Jason could see that there was very little meat on the bones underneath her uniform. "You are right. Your world was populated by our race. We brought you to this system when our planets became overcrowded. A series of cataclysms occurred after the people were placed here. An asteroid broke the canopy that protected your planet from the UV rays of your sun. Parts of the population survived and we brought in people from other worlds to increase the population."

"Then that explains the different races?"

"Yes, it does. We played with the mix until we thought we had it right."

"Right for who? Were you the ones who introduced us to the concept of a Supreme Being?"

Angat nodded sadly. "Yes, we did. Understand that we had to bring you as quickly as we possibly could to a level of technology where you could make up your minds for yourselves. Introducing religion into the existing societies was a natural link to bring about the fruition of our plans."

Jason felt the ire rising in his cheeks. "You should have left us alone! You know that we've had nothing but heartache, pestilence and war since you meddled with us. And most of that was in the name of religion!"

"Please, Commander. Settle down and listen. This was done in the dim past and your race has progressed to the point where you are almost ready to venture out into space. That would not have happened if we hadn't turned your thoughts inward so that you could discover who you truly are. I may not have taken the same tack on the problem of your education from jockeying camels to flying spacecraft, but I came along long after your destiny was set."

Again Jason had considerable difficulty keeping the anger out of his voice. "You speak of our destiny as if it were cut in stone."

Her thin shoulders lifted. "You do have a destiny of sorts, Commander. You as a people will burst into space to take your place with the other races that populate known space. That is what I mean by destiny. You will fulfill yours, I assure you."

"You seem to be pretty certain of that, but that's not why I'm here, is it?"

Angat gazed at the screen. "No, that isn't the reason you are here," she turned toward him after a moment. "You are here because you got placed in harm's way by your people and used as bait to bring the situation on Mars to a point where we can get rid of their civilization with a measure of success."

That sunk in for a while. "Did you plan it, or did our people?"

"It was completely on your own, I assure you. We haven't visited this sector for over ten thousand of your years. But we've been trying to eradicate the species you met in Bartam for many of your centuries and this is one of the worst infestations we've encountered."

"Why the animosity?"

Angat looked deeply into Jason's eyes. "I must impress on you. The race that Bartam comes from only knows one way of getting something – taking it by force. Across the galaxy they are hunted and pursued. We were not aware that they were here until after we had planted you on Earth. We would never have placed you here if we had known. Now it is time to take care of that mistake."

"What are you going to do?" Jason asked quietly.

"Commander, we are going to use the weapons that Bartam transported here and take out the upper crust of their society. After that we are going to turn the pursuit of eradication over to you."

"To me? Why me?"

"Because you have been altered to survive the harsh climatic changes that Mars goes through. You may not realize this, Commander, but you are a new species. And you have several others down there on the planet who are the same as you."

That took a while to sink in and she let him think. Finally, "But I want to go back to my family on Earth and live a normal life."

"And you know that that is not an option, Commander. And you know why, don't you?"

Jason had to admit that he did and she continued, "If you come anywhere near your planet you will infect people with the same thing that you have. You will completely change the face of your society and, this is important, Commander. You will become as hunted as those down there on the planet are hunted now. I think you have dreams that one-day your sons and daughters will travel to the stars. They cannot do it with that virus in their blood. It must die on Mars."

Her statement was as blunt as it could be. Jason sat back and considered what he had heard. "I guess there is no way to get a second opinion on this one, is there?"

Angat sadly shook her head. "This is the one you'll have to trust me on, Jason."

"You understand that I've come to trust no one in the last couple months."

"Yes, we understand that very well. But you are going to have to step up to the plate and take this one on your shoulders."

Jason stared back at Angat. "What if I refuse?"

"Then your body will be discovered inside the Pegasus and we will continue working on the problem with the other crew-members. It's just that you happen to be the best candidate we have to complete this with."

"Looks like we got a job to do, but let me ask this. Will we be given a full measure of life on Mars and will our children be allowed back into mainstream humanity at some point in the future?"

"Sadly, Commander, I can't answer those questions. I would say you will have opportunity for a full life on Mars, but I don't know that we can ever remove the virus from your bodies. We have tried that in the past and can only promise you that we will try. Is that answer enough for you?"

"I guess it will have to do. When do we begin?"

"Immediately. We don't have much time to waste. I'm going to give you a full briefing before things break open, so hold onto your straps." She extended her hand to Jason. "Welcome aboard, Commander."

Jason smiled grimly. "I sure hope this is going to be worth it."

33 THE DEVICE

Amadeus strode into the throne room and immediately felt his self-confidence wither as a cold spot developed in his middle. His King was doing some striding of his own around a series of objects that had appeared in the center of the room.

His eyes met Amadeus' and he went berserk. "You told me these things were contained, Amadeus," he pointed a bony claw in the direction of his advisor. "Explain to me why they suddenly appeared here."

As Amadeus was carefully considering his reply one of the devices beeped. Both men jumped, the King ending up behind his throne, staring out. Amadeus walked over to the offending instrument and looked at the faceplate.

Large orange symbols blinked on the console. He couldn't be certain what they said, but he knew a countdown when he saw one. He looked up as King Leopold touched his shoulder.

"Your Majesty, I suggest you leave immediately. This device is going to explode!"

"How much time do we have? And don't bother lying to me this time, Amadeus. I should have taken your miserable head when you did that the first time. Next time I won't be so apt to trust anyone."

Amadeus smiled grimly and tried to decipher the human symbols. The humans had the same number of digits as he did, so he made an educated guess.

"I'd say you aren't going to have to worry about trusting anyone else, your Majesty. We have less than ten minutes to make our escape and there is no way that we can get far enough away from this to do us any good. So take my head if that will do any good, but I suggest we just sit down and talk of this and that while we wait."

Leopold took a long glance at his companion and shrugged. Amadeus had never, that he knew of anyway, intentionally lied to him. "Where did they come from? Did the humans deliver them from their space probes?"

Amadeus shook his head as he inspected the packs. "No. This one is the exact one that Bartam was wearing." He pointed at a scratch he had placed himself on the pack after Bartam had taken it off.

"Someone wanted to insure we were taken out by these devices and I've seen nothing in the human's arsenal that suggests they can do what you suggest. They don't have that level of technology yet."

"They who?" Leopold walked over and sat upon his throne. "Who does have the technology?"

"The only ones I can think of is the Denebians, but we haven't heard anything from them in so long that we had thought them maybe extinct," since there was no chair other than the throne in the room, Amadeus sat on the edge of the raised platform and looked up at his King. "I think we've underestimated them."

"And who is going to pay for that, Amadeus?"

"Well, I guess we both will," he raised his eyes to meet Leopold's. Then it dawned on him that they weren't the only ones who would perish.

"Yes, advisor. I see that you see it now. We have moved all of our people to this facility so they wouldn't be blown to hell by the explosion you had planned. Now they are as much at risk as we are. Do you suppose we should sound a warning?"

Amadeus sadly shook his head. "No, Sire. They wouldn't have time to do anything but panic. Leave them a little dignity to the minutes remaining of their lives."

Leopold finally smiled. "Yes, of course. Just think, Amadeus, I don't have to wait for another cycle to have the terrible burden of managing this fractious people lifted from my shoulders. I won't have to wake up in the morning dreading the day's drudgery."

Crossing his legs under him, Amadeus tried to relax, but his mind was going at supersonic pace. "I have to know why..."

Within his cell, Bartam was pacing the short distance from wall to wall. His blood was beginning to boil. Amadeus should have returned by now. He wanted nothing more than to get his hands around Leopold's throat. Amadeus was going to arrange that. He screamed in frustration and struck out at the walls until his hands were bloodied. All he could do then was look at them.

Jason materialized inside Michelle's cell. His body tingled as all the elements settled back into their required places. He still didn't know how he felt about being torn to shreds in one place and reconstituted up arrival at another point.

What if the reconstituting computer made an error of a couple inches? He might have found himself knee deep in bedrock. But the computer hadn't made a mistake. Jason looked at his watch and almost panicked. He had less than five minutes to find her and get out.

He looked around the cell furiously. Did she get out? He was about to think so when he saw a boot sticking around the edge of a platform that divided the cell in half. He hurriedly moved around the platform and went down to his knees. Michelle was facing the pedestal. Jason had to turn her over. Sand covered her lips. He brushed it off and lowered his head to her chest. He could hear a faint heartbeat.

'Commander, this is Anwar. I'm detecting that you've found your crewmember. Are you ready to beam out?'

'Yes. And get us out of here fast. We don't have much time. I really don't want to add radioactivity to this virus I'm carrying.'

'Stand back from her. I'm going to beam her directly to our sickbay. Don't worry, Commander. I've never lost anyone in the beam.' The connection broke suddenly as Michelle's body began to gleam and then disappeared.

Jason looked around the cell and leaned against the pedestal. He watched as his hands became translucent. He could see the rock through them. Then he was standing beside Arwar.

"Angat wants to see you on the bridge immediately. Follow me." She moved faster than he had seen any of them move before. When he stepped onto the bridge Angat looked up and indicated the cloud that was already rising from the surface of Mars.

"That could become a real hazard for your group, Commander. We can't clean it up and you are going to have fallout from it for a while. But we have found a place near the southern pole region where you can weather the storms this upheaval is going to cause. We predict a new volcano is going to rival your Olympus Mons for a while." She fell silent for several moments, then continued.

"Commander, we rescued your other crewmembers and have already transported them to the place I spoke of. We want you to succeed and to prosper. But you know why we can't come right out and give you direct aid."

Jason nodded. "Yes, I know that you have to empower us to do things on our own. I understand that. What I don't think I'll ever understand is why you didn't tell us we were your children in the first place."

Angat looked at him a long time before she finally answered. "Because we have had much experience with transplanting people on new planets. If the colonists think they are only a colony – they fail. If they believe they originated on the planet – they bond with it and make it their own. It's a simple matter of knowing there isn't any other place to go."

Jason felt a tickle in the back of his mind. Michelle's voice was suddenly reverberating in his head. He almost screamed for her to turn down the volume. 'I'm here.'

'Jason. Thank God! Jason, they were going to leave me in that cell to die. Where am I?'

'You are in a hospital bay so just lie back and relax. We are on a ship standing off in space above Mars. I was able to get you out and will explain things to you later. Just relax and try to get some sleep. Your body needs it.'

Michelle could feel herself slipping back into unconsciousness. 'You will be here when I wake up?'

'I will be there when you wake up.' He felt her connection fade and turned back to Angat. "Is our connection to each other a product of the virus or something entirely different?"

"We aren't sure where you picked it up, Commander. We think the Martians probably developed it for long distance communications after their ecology went bust. We don't know if that is a trait that passed to you with the virus. Commander, Anwar is ready to go over a list of things she will transfer to your new quarters. We will leave you with some supplies and equipment that will help you develop your community into a viable place to live."

Jason turned to leave, but then thought of something. "And the virus eradicator? What of that? And how do we kill the feral Martians when we meet them?"

Angat's eyes bored into Jason's from across the room. "You will have to figure that out for yourself. You have your job to do, Commander. Now go and do it." She turned away from him and Jason couldn't help but think how absolutely sad she appeared. "We will do it, Angat. We will do it."

From orbit Jason witnessed the tremendous explosion. Amanda had indeed souped up the three devices. Sand and debris lifted high into the thin atmosphere and started settling back onto the planet.

"We are really going to have trouble with that for a while," he stated flatly. He watched as sheer winds in the upper atmosphere ripped the outer edges of the nuclear cloud to shreds. There was going to be no place on the planet that wouldn't be touched by it.

Arnak stepped into the control room and got his attention. "Are you ready to leave, Commander?"

Jason took one last look at the fused, blackened impact crater that could now be seen through the thinning debris and nodded. He stood in front of Arnak and handed her a message he had written for Angat. She placed it inside her tunic and motioned for him to follow.

Going from astronaut to ground pounder was not Jason's idea of a good progression in job titles. But he had a job to do. Maybe someday his children's children could complete their destiny with the rest of Earth's humanity.

34 RESOLUTION

Angat of Deneb glanced again at the letter that had been handed to her. Sadness coursed through her frail body as she thought of all the crimes against humanity that had been perpetrated by the desire to expedite the development of the culture on Earth. But she had been correct.

The decision wasn't hers. She had come along long after those decisions. She couldn't change anything that had been done, but her shoulders sagged as she considered Earth's situation. She read further.

"Angat, we as a people may not want to join your confederation once we arrive at what you call our bursting out place. Think of all that we've gone through on our way to maturity. Brother has killed brother, whole races have been purged and decimated, ethnic cleansing is still not considered taboo and we look at each other with extreme suspicion because of our skin color.

How do you think we can join you when our past is littered with all that baggage? We can barely tolerate ourselves. Just because we come charging out into space with our newfound technology doesn't mean that your people will open their arms for us. After meeting you, I can see that now.

We could have done without all the chest beating; I AM your God fiction. You should have just come out and told us where we are really from. Non-technological man might not have been accepting of that, but it would have been much better for us in the long run.

We shouldn't have to 'out-grow' our dependence on you. We should have been empowered by you. Even when we do join you – we will probably still be dependent on you. I don't see what benefit you are going to derive from the human race developed upon Earth.

Please pass on to the General that I don't appreciate the way he used me and my crew to bring about the fruition of your plan. He should have told you to shove it! Don't come back to Mars thinking that a docile society will be awaiting your arrival."

Angat put the letter onto the console in front of her. "He doesn't understand," was all she could think to say. But she had seen the future.

ABOUT THE AUTHOR

Tim Conley really began writing at the young age of six when he would recount his daydreams to whoever would listen. His authoritarian father discouraged this and any other action that smelled of books and reading. Tim would sneak into any hidden away corner and escape through the avenue of reading and was known as a loner and dreamer by his classmates, preferring his own company and that of 'made-up characters' to that of friends. Now at age 60, Tim has a huge amount of material to draw from to create his own settings and characters.

Tim is still a loner, living in San Jose, California with his wife and lover, Carmela Santos (a teacher from the Philippines). He would like to run a small ranch with a couple horses, some pigs and chickens.

Tim is satisfied to live the quiet life of a simple man. He studied writing at the University College at Memphis State University. The fact is he enjoys writing more than all the other things he has accomplished in life. Teaching for inner city schools has provided excitement in his life, but he has configured a quiet place where he can sit at the computer during the evening to recount his 'thoughts of the day...dream.'

Tales From Avalon is not the first and only writing that Tim has done. Tim also has TRANSDEM, INC. and The Curse of Indian Gold that were published by Brandywine Books and PublishAmerica respectively. He is currently working on a four volume space opera named Journey to Mars, Memoirs of a Country boy, Crystal Possession: Vanessa's Story, Crystal Possession: Imagination Island and Dark Moons on Chimera, A One-Way Trip and Imagination Island.

Other titles by this author include:

Sci-fi category:
TRANSDEM, Inc., Omegan Arrival
Crystal Possession: Vanessa's Story
Journey to Mars: The Awakening
Journey to Mars: Blood is Forever
Journey to Mars: To Fight the Evil
Tales from Avalon
Avalon, Book 1 – The Avalonian Connection *
Avalon, Book 2 – Genesis: To Outrun a Nova *
Avalon, Book 3 – The Toltec Expedition *
Avalon, Book 4 – The Chen Lao Conspiracy *
Avalon, Book 5 – The Oludavi Revelation *
Avalon, Book 6 – 2013: The Melting Pot *
Avalon, Book 7 – 2023: Life Here After *

Horror category:
The Curse of Indian Gold
A Tale of Cardiff Glen

Fantasy:
Dark Moons on Chimera: Birth under a Sign *

Biography/Poetry category:
Memoirs of a Country boy
Poetic License
Thunder Breaks in on Silence
Short Stories, Essays and Comments

How-to category:
Writing 101: For Beginners

Screenplays:
A Screenplay: Immoral Authority

*Published as e-Books at Smashwords.com

Made in the USA
Charleston, SC
26 September 2012